Jack & Coke

D1713890

The Uncertain Saints MC- Book 2

LANI LYNN VALE

Lani Lynn Vale

**ISBN-13:
978-1532766985**

**ISBN-10:
153276698X**

Dedication

I've done a lot of growing over the last three years that I've been self-published, and each of those three years I've made many new friends in my book world. So many people I only know by names and Facebook profile pictures, and each of you have made a huge impact on my life. You've kept me writing when all I want to do is take a break. You've offered encouragement, and overall had a huge impact on my life. So this book is dedicated to the ladies that have made a point to take time out of there day to tell me how much they've loved my books. Thank you all so much, and know that this wouldn't be possible without y'all.

Acknowledgements

Golden Czermak AKA Furiousfotog- I don't know if you have any idea just how awesome you are, but I'm here to tell you that you're just that. Super awesome. Your photos are by far my favorites. Thank you for sharing your work with the world.

Nick Bennett- when I saw this photo of you, I knew you'd be perfect for Mig. Thank you so much for allowing this photo to be taken. It's beautiful, and so are you.

Dani- you sure do know how to make my pretties shine. You have no idea how much I adore you.

CONTENTS

Other Titles by Lani Lynn Vale:

The Freebirds

Boomtown

Highway Don't Care

Another One Bites the Dust

Last Day of My Life

Texas Tornado

I Don't Dance

The Heroes of The Dixie Wardens MC

Lights To My Siren

Halligan To My Axe

Kevlar To My Vest

Keys To My Cuffs

Life To My Flight

Charge To My Line

Code 11- KPD SWAT Series

Center Mass

Double Tap

Bang Switch

Execution Style

Charlie Foxtrot

Kill Shot

Coup De Grace

The Uncertain Saints MC

Whiskey Neat

Jack & Coke

Kilgore Fire

Shock Advised

Flash Point

CHAPTER 1

*Don't try to tell me that hungry is not an emotion. I feel that shit
in my soul.*
-Annie to Mig

Mig

I stepped out of my house, clad only in a pair of jeans and nothing else,
and slowly started towards my neighbor's house.

I'd been in the kitchen, taking a sip of some orange juice straight from
the jug, when I'd looked over to see two black-clad figures entering the
back of my neighbor's house.

My neighbor that was a woman.

A very beautiful woman.

Instead of walking around to the back, I went to Annie's window, the
one that was directly across from mine, and slowly entered it.

Most people didn't realize we kept our windows open since our houses
were so close together.

Which was a good thing, too, since the intruders had thought it better to
go through the back of the house instead of this easier to access window.

If they'd done that, I would've never seen them until it was too late...*if
at all.*

The moment my feet touched down on Annie's hardwood floor, I moved
silently over to the bed where she slept soundly.

My hand covered her mouth, and she startled awake like a scalded cat.

She tried to scream behind my hand, but I moved onto the bed until I could flatten my body on top of hers.

The air left her lungs in a rush the moment I gave her all of my body weight.

"Shhh," I said, barely audible against her ear. "It's Mig. You're okay."

Annie immediately went limp.

"Where's your dog?" I asked, removing my hand.

"In her cage," she answered almost tonelessly.

As I listened to her, my heart started to pound for a completely different reason at feeling her soft body underneath mine.

"I'm going to go check your house. Call 911. Don't speak. They'll trace your call and dispatch units. Get off the bed and go to the corner of the room beside the dresser," I pointed in the direction I wanted her to go.

She nodded against my chest. Reluctantly, I moved up and over the bed, finally stopping at the door.

With the utmost care, I opened the door and started to move down the hall.

I could hear the scuffle of feet now, but not much more than that.

Following the sounds to the living room, I paused at the corner of the mouth of the hall and aimed my gun at the uninvited guests.

"Freeze," I said, menace leeching out of my steely voice.

The flashlights stopped bobbing around and both men froze.

"Put your hands behind by your head and link your fingers," I ordered.

They both complied.

I moved slowly to the side of them, keeping them in my line of sight, as I stopped in front of the light switch and hit the lights.

Both men, dressed in black, with their masks up around their foreheads, blinked at the suddenness of the light switching on.

I recognized the one on the left instantly.

He was Annie's screw up ex-husband.

I'd met him at the diner in town when he'd tried to sit down at the booth that Annie had been occupying.

In her haste to get away from him, she'd bumped into me as I made my way to a table with my wife.

I'd caught her before she'd hit the ground, and immediately turned to put Annie at my back, allowing me to place my body in between her and her ex-husband.

He hadn't liked that much, and I'd made a friend and an enemy all in one day.

My wife already hated the fact that I was a 'protector' by nature and had made sure to let me know she didn't appreciate me having my hands on another woman. Regardless of the circumstances.

Annie had instantly liked me, extremely happy that she'd finally found a man she could count on.

And Mr. Autrey, Annie's ex-husband, had made sure to harass me every chance he got.

"What are you doing in my wife's house?" Ross Autrey snapped at me.

I raised an eyebrow at him.

"I could ask you the same thing," I answered instead.

Ross narrowed his eyes at me, and I smirked.

"Go on," I goaded, smiling congenially at him. "Try it. Make my day."

Ross proved he wasn't stupid.

The friend with him, however, proved he was.

He let his hands slowly slip from his head, and I laughed.

"Ross. How about you tell your friend how good of a shot I am," I invited.

Ross turned his head in the direction of his friend, and shook his head, whispering frantically at him. "Don't move, man. He's gonna blow your head apart."

The friend saw the error in his ways, *luckily*.

"Annie," I called. "Tell the cops there are two intruders. One is your ex, and the other is…"

I looked at the man.

"Howard. Howard Ryan," he replied grudgingly.

"You got that?" I called.

"Yes!" Annie called from the bedroom.

Hopefully she was still in her spot, but it sounded to me like she'd been closer than I wanted her to be right then.

And I knew she wouldn't spend much more time hidden away.

"Go get the door for the policemen I can see outside," I called. "And tell them you have a DEA Agent in your house so they don't try to shoot me when they enter."

"I already did," I heard Annie say as she got closer.

I saw her for only a few seconds before she disappeared around the edge of the hallway into the entry way beyond it.

Then the door was unchained, unlocked and swung open.

Three cops were the next to enter, and I nodded at the one I knew.

"Hey there, Officer Kirkpatrick," I called to my good friend.

We had drinks every week, sometimes multiple times a week.

I had to do some creative maneuvering to get away from my wife, and Officer Kirkpatrick, a.k.a. Bullseye, was one of my moves.

Well, I didn't do him…but I hung out with him.

Often.

And Bullseye had a hell of a wife that didn't care if I was over there as much as I was.

"What's shakin'?" Bullseye asked.

"These two men here decided to break into Annie's house. I'm just here making sure that they don't get off with anything valuable," I answered.

The other officer, Antonio Juarez, I didn't know very well.

He was new, and hung out with the young'uns instead of us old folks.

Well, I was thirty-four, which wasn't 'old' per se, but it sure as fuck wasn't young, either.

"What's that in his hand?" Juarez asked.

I looked down at Howard Ryan's hand, and narrowed my eyes.

"That's Annie's purse," I answered.

Annie's 'purse' was more of a beach bag, and I didn't know how the hell she found anything in it.

But I wouldn't know what to do with her if she didn't have it with her.

She'd been able to supply me with an ice pack, and a water on two different occasions, so I wasn't one to complain when it was beneficial to me.

"Well, boys, let's go for a ride downtown," Bullseye said, walking behind Howard Ryan and handcuffing him.

Ryan shot me an evil look as he left, promising retribution, and I smiled at him.

Bring it, little boy. You can't handle this, my look said.

Forty-five minutes later, the cops were leaving with both men in the back of two separate cars, and I was left standing on Annie's front porch with her next to me.

"Thank you," she said, looking up at me with all sorts of promises in her eyes.

I touched my fingertips to her cheek and smiled down at her.

God, she was beautiful.

Long, wavy brown hair that went down to her mid back. Beautiful, full lips.

A smokin' ass.

Light bronze skin that was nearly the color of mine.

She wasn't Italian like me, though.

She was Puerto Rican, and she wouldn't let anyone call her otherwise.

I'd give anything to be with her but my life, and name, belonged to my wife.

God, if there was any way I could rewind a year, I'd do it in a heartbeat.

I would've never invited my now wife, Jennifer, to the club party.

Jennifer was the exact opposite of Annie.

Rude, opinionated and selfish.

Now she was six months pregnant with my child, and I hated every fucking second of my life.

"You're welcome," I said roughly. "I'm gonna have a few men over here in the next few days to install an alarm and make sure nobody can ever do that to you again."

"Mig, what the ever loving fuck are you doing over there?" My wife screeched.

I winced and slowly dropped my hand, looking over at Jennifer like one would a pile of fish heads and vomit.

Then I turned around when I saw she was dressed in little to nothing.

How *not* surprising.

The woman didn't know what the fuck clothes were.

I'd get home in the evenings from work, and she'd be wearing clothes that revealed her ass, her breasts and belly.

And honestly, for a six-month pregnant woman, she looked great.

But nobody needed to see that.

And I hated that she went out in the front yard to 'greet' me when I got home from work.

What she was really doing was trying to make me jealous.

Little did she know, I couldn't get jealous of any other man when it came to her.

I would have to care about her first, and I didn't.

And I'd give her up in a heartbeat if she wasn't having my kid.

"Be safe. Make sure you lock your doors," I ordered Annie.

I saw the pity on her face as I turned and walked down her front walk, crossing through her yard into my own.

I walked into the house, completely ignoring the fact that Jennifer was still looking at me with suspicion in her eyes.

I'd never cheat on her, but she constantly accused me of it.

"Annie's house was broken into," I said by way of explanation as I made it to the kitchen.

I grabbed a beer.

And just in time, too.

"I can't fucking believe that you left me here to go save another woman," my wife hissed at me.

I narrowed my eyes on my beer bottle as a thousand different things went through my ears at once.

I can't believe you trapped me into marrying you.

I can't believe you gave me a date rape drug to make me fuck you.

I can't believe we now have a baby on the way and I can't fucking leave because my morals don't allow me to leave a woman that's carrying my child.

I can't believe you think I care even a single bit about you. If you weren't carrying my child, I could give any less of a crap about you.

I didn't answer her.

Instead, I stayed quiet, even though every inch of my being wanted to yell at her...tear her apart with my words.

I slept next to the woman every single fucking night, and my skin crawled the entire time.

Instead, I stayed awake and watched the window beyond my room, wishing it was Annie in bed with me instead of the woman currently looking at me like I'd skinned her pet rabbit in front of her eyes.

I flipped on the TV once I reached the living room, ignoring Jennifer and the fact that it was nearly four AM.

I had to be up in less than an hour anyway, so what was the point of trying to go back to bed?

Then again, I hadn't slept well in over four months since I'd married Jennifer.

"Are you just going to fucking ignore me for the rest of the night?" She hissed.

I finally looked away from the TV, unaware what was even on, and stared at her.

"Go away."

Jennifer narrowed her eyes.

"You're my husband, I can talk to you whenever I fuckin' want to," she murmured.

I narrowed my eyes at her.

"That's crass. Stop talking like a piece of trash and leave me alone," I growled, turning my eyes back to the TV.

"I don't even know why I married you. I should divorce you," she hissed.

I wish you would. Then I'd be off the hook.

She wouldn't do that, though.

Not with my father being who he was.

What Jennifer saw was dollar signs, meaning she would never leave.

I smiled to myself.

What she didn't know was that I couldn't touch my money until I was forty years of age.

I kept my accounts to myself, too.

I paid for Jennifer's doctor bills, the house note, all the utility bills and food.

What I didn't pay for were Jennifer's clothes, her car note, nor her credit card bills.

I'd also made her sign a pre-nup that was not only iron clad, but it gave her absolutely nothing.

Nothing.

And the first time she cheated, she'd get slapped with a custody suit a mile wide.

And she *would* cheat.

It was only a matter of time.

I didn't expect it to happen yet, seeing as how she was pregnant with my kid, but I wouldn't put it past her to try.

Nobody in this town would do her, though.

She'd have to go find it somewhere where everyone didn't know me.

"I wish you didn't treat me so badly. I'm your wife and the mother of your child," she hissed.

I looked back at her.

"And how did you get to be that again? Was it my beer that you dropped the drug in, or my Jack and Coke?" I challenged.

She snapped her mouth shut, knowing when it was time to shut up and leave.

Which was good for her, because I was about to fuckin' lose it.

She left with a stomp of her feet, and I smiled.

Goddamn that woman was a piece of work.

I turned back to the TV, groaning when Annie's commercial came on.

God, now that woman was somethin'.

She was a fuckin' beauty, and I'd give my left nut to have her.

"Come down and visit me," my Annie on the commercial smiled at the camera. *"I'll give you a massage and style that you'll love."*

Maybe a massage was in my future.

Lani Lynn Vale

CHAPTER 2

Almost every hand you've ever shaken has had a dick in it at some point.
-Proven Fact

Mig

"Can you repeat that? I don't think I heard you quite right," I said into the mic I had in my hand.

I was working a case with the local Sheriff's Department, and I was currently about five minutes away from the only diner in town to get food.

Something I'd told to about three sheriff's deputies, one of those being my good friend, and MC brother, Ridley.

Ridley was a member of the Uncertain Saints with me. He'd also been one of the men that'd recruited me for the club.

"I said, there's a man wielding a chain saw at the diner. I'm asking you to be cautious when you go," Ridley replied seriously.

I pinched the bridge of my nose with my forefinger and thumb, and sighed.

"Got it," I said, pulling into the driveway that would lead me down to the diner.

The diner was located on Uncertain's claim to fame, The Caddo River.

I dropped the mic into its holder and got out of my company issued truck.

I was a DEA agent stationed in Uncertain, Texas.

The Caddo River was also the reason I was here as an agent.

Caddo was a hotbed of drug and firearm transport activity.

After about four major busts within two weeks of each other, the DEA opened a satellite office in the little town of Uncertain.

The DEA and the Texas Rangers were on a joint task force that was commissioned to combat the drug and firearm trade that was taking over this small town. Although it'd slowed down since we'd started it, there was still a lot of work to do.

Movement in my peripheral vision had me turning in time to see Griffin, a fellow member of the Uncertain Saints, as well as one of the Texas Rangers on the joint taskforce, walking toward me.

"See you're in that cage instead of on your bike," Griffin said, swinging his leg over his bike to dismount.

"My boss got upset with me that I had a 'perfectly good company vehicle' that I wasn't using," I answered as we both walked around to the back of the diner.

"You know about the chainsaw wielder?" I asked.

Griffin nodded. "Heard it on my scanner," he said, indicating the portable radio on his belt.

When he was on his bike, he had to take the portable radio since it didn't have a scanner like his company-issued vehicle did.

Something I did as well when I was on my bike.

I took the issued vehicle every couple of days to make my boss think I was using it.

Mostly I hated it, and usually tried to take my bike since riding in a cage made me feel closed in and claustrophobic.

See, I was an adrenaline junkie, and nothing gave me more of a rush than flying a F-16 through the sky at Mach 2.

The closest I could get to that feeling was riding my bike at over a hundred miles an hour. Sure, it wasn't fifteen hundred miles an hour like I could do in the air, but it was nothing to sneeze at either.

I nodded, and we both made our way into the back door of the diner that led into the kitchen.

"You're gonna go get him, right?" Elton, the cook for the diner, asked.

I nodded and pushed the kitchen door open slightly to see what was going on, and froze.

A familiar woman with dark brown hair, a very distinctive tattoo on her shoulder, from collarbone to elbow, of a peacock, and a look of death in her eyes, reared back and slammed the napkin holder over the man wielding the chainsaw's head.

The chainsaw dropped to the floor with a clatter, sputtering for a short time before the engine finally died.

The diner was completely silent as the man who'd had the chainsaw in his hands turned around with a look of rage in his eyes.

"Freeze," I said to the man as he reared back his hand to strike out at Annie.

Annie didn't look scared in the least as she backed away from the man whose fist was still raised.

And then even further until her back was against the counter

I wanted to reach out and touch her.

My hands practically burned with the urge, *but I didn't.*

Instead, I moved around the counter and placed my body in front of hers, protecting her from another man that wanted to do her harm for the second time in less than twenty-four hours.

"Put your hands behind your head," I ordered.

I sounded like a fuckin' broken record.

First this morning, then this afternoon.

The chainsaw wielder raised his hands part of the way up, albeit very reluctantly.

"Turn the fuck around and put your hands on your fuckin' head!"

Obviously, he wasn't moving fast enough for Griffin's liking, because at Griffin's shouted order, the man jumped, turned and placed his hands all the way on top of his head.

Griffin had him cuffed in seconds, and I finally replaced my weapon in the holster under my arm.

"Nice swing," I said, tossing that comment over my shoulder at Annie.

Annie's brilliant smile lit up the fuckin' room.

"My father taught me everything I know," she responded cheekily.

I winked at her and turned around, addressing Francine behind the counter.

"Can you make me and Griffin a burger and fries to go?" I asked her.

She blinked, then nodded slowly.

She was one of the oldest waitresses I'd ever seen, but she was damn fine at her job.

She reminded me a lot of my grandmother, and I couldn't wait to introduce my Nonnie to her.

They'd get along famously.

I'd been stationed in Uncertain, Texas for well a while now, and not once had I convinced her to come down.

"As soon as you get yourself a fine woman, I'll come," was always my Nonnie's answer.

My Nonnie had yet to meet my wife, and I hoped she never had to.

I planned on taking our child up to visit Nonnie and my mother the week he or she was born.

What I didn't plan on doing was taking Jennifer with me.

I knew it'd be a fight, but I didn't really care at this point.

Even the thought of my Nonnie being in Jennifer's presence made my stomach churn.

My Nonnie was what you would call soft-hearted.

She loved everyone and everything.

I had no doubt that Jennifer would get my Nonnie to love her.

Jennifer was a manipulative bitch, and she'd use absolutely anything to get closer to me.

To sink her claws in further.

"You should go into the protection business or something," Annie supplied as I turned to survey the room.

I looked down at her twinkling eyes, and snorted.

"You do know I'm a DEA agent, right?" I asked.

She nodded.

"I guessed you were by the shirts I see you wearing on your way to work," she teased.

She was out in her yard every morning watering; I saw her every morning as I left.

It wasn't a surprise that she knew what I wore to work.

"Here you are," Francine said from behind me.

"What the hell?" I asked.

It took them less than three minutes to get it done.

"It's on the house, too. I snagged another order so you wouldn't have to wait any longer," Francine explained.

I nodded.

"Oh, okay. Thank you," I acknowledged.

Francine smiled a little wobbly.

"You deserve that and so much more," she said emphatically.

***

Annie

I watched Mig talk to Griffin as surreptitiously as I could.

"What are you looking at?" My sister, Tasha, asked me.

I tilted my head in the direction of Mig and Griffin.

"The one on the left. With the tight black jeans and black t-shirt that says DEA on the breast pocket," I whispered.

My sister's eyes went to Mig, and she smiled.

"That's your neighbor, isn't it?" She confirmed.

I nodded. "Yeah, that's him."

"Who's the other guy?" Tasha asked.

I glanced quickly in their direction, then turned back to my cold burger and limp French fries.

"The other one is Griffin Storm. He's married to Lenore, you remember her, right?" I asked.

"She's the one that owns Uncertain Pleasures, correct?" She said, popping a cherry tomato in her mouth and looking at me with a raised brow.

I nodded in confirmation. "Yeah."

I'd met Lenore when she was dating Griffin and then became friends when I'd bought my shop that was directly next to her sex toy shop, Uncertain Pleasures.

We'd hit it off, and now we swapped services.

I cut Lenore's hair, or gave her a massage, in exchange for her giving me free sex toys.

Or condoms.

Or anything I wanted, really.

I'd not moved beyond the former two, though.

I was too chicken to try any of the more adventurous stuff without having that little push in the right direction. And without the right man, that would never happen.

"I thought you said Mig was married," my sister asked.

I looked up at her. "He is."

She gave me a questioning look.

"Then why is he looking at you like he wants to eat you alive, one slow, luxurious lick at a time?" She questioned.

You know those times that you know you shouldn't look?

Like, with everything in your being you want to look, but you know if you do, you'll be caught looking?

Well, I was caught looking.

And I liked it.

The way his eyes met mine made me feel like we were the only ones in the entire diner instead of it being filled with nearly fifty people.

He held my eyes for a long time.

So long that I knew it would be considered more than just a glance.

The only thing a married man should be doing, anyway.

"Maybe he's not happily married," Tasha offered when Mig finally looked away from me.

I shrugged.

"She yells at him a lot, and he just takes it. I don't know if they're happy or not, but I know from what I can see, it isn't all sunshine and roses," I answered, trying in vain not to look back at Mig.

Except when I did, he was leaving, and I was left feeling bereft.

I watched the muscles in his back play with the movement of his arms.

Watched the muscles bunch as he reached his arm forward and pushed open the diner's door.

Then I licked my lips as I watched him walk to the SUV that I hadn't seen until now and drop in it.

I'd have had to climb into it.

But Mig was tall.

Really tall.

At least six foot three or more.

He rolled his window down and looked in the direction of the diner once more, and my breath caught when his eyes met mine.

He smiled.

A quick, almost imperceptible flash, but I saw it.

And I blushed.

His grin got wider.

How he could even see that from where he was, I didn't know. But I knew he knew what he did to me.

With one last look, he slipped a pair of shades over his eyes that reminded me of the ones baseball players wore, the sporty type where the lens came to a point at their cheekbones.

They covered up his beautiful gray eyes that always reminded me of storm clouds. Then he placed his heavily tattooed arm on the door, and started to back out of the parking spot.

I watched until I couldn't see him any longer.

"Oh, you've got it bad," Tasha teased.

I returned my gaze to her.

"He's married," I answered with a sigh.

She nodded. "Well, from what I could tell, y'all definitely have some chemistry going on. But you need to be careful, because that's exactly what your new business does not need: you being known as a home wrecker."

I snorted.

"The man's a biker…isn't it expected that he'd cheat?" I asked, pushing away the basket containing my lunch.

My stomach was in knots as I thought about him being married.

Tasha was right though, I totally had the hots for him.

And I'd had them for a long time.

I'd been in Uncertain, Texas for going on six years now.

My parents had moved here at the end of my senior year.

My father had just gotten out of the military, and he'd decided to open a fishing and bait shop off the side of Caddo Lake.

So I'd been here the day Mig had arrived in town.

He'd ridden in on his Harley, dressed in a black leather jacket, tight faded blue jeans, and his signature wraparound sunglasses.

And here I was, years later, still just as hot for him as the day I'd seen him for the first time.

I'd never told anyone about my avid crush on Mig, though.

I was too scared of all that was him.

Secretly, I was worried that if I admitted my crush, he'd somehow find out.

He was good like that.

Then I'd moved into the house next to him, completely by accident, and about died.

But he'd been exceptionally cool about everything.

And he'd become a friend, even if from a distance.

A friend that I had the hots for…who was married…with a kid on the way.

Yeah, *fuck my life.*

CHAPTER 3

Ladies, if you see a man eating BBQ wings with a knife and fork, it's likely he doesn't eat pussy right either. Run. Don't look back. You can thank me later.
-Tasha to Annie on the eve of her marriage to Ross

Annie

Ross: I think about you every day.

Me: I think about pizza every day.

Ross: Don't you miss me even a little bit?

Me: Let me think about it.

Ross: Well?

Me: Well, what?

Ross: Do you miss me?

Me: No.

Ross: Not even a little bit?

I thought about that for a second.

Did I miss him at all?

No.

Did I miss being with someone?

Yes.

31

Would I take Ross back to get *that* back?

Hell fucking no.

Me: No.

I placed my phone down onto the coffee table, then turned my head to study my front yard.

It'd been mowed.

By Mig, no doubt.

Jesus, did the man ever slow down?

I wished I'd have gotten up the courage to talk to him when I'd first moved in.

Then Ross would've never happened.

And I might be happy right now, living the life his wife was living instead of my miserable excuse for an existence.

I stood up when I saw Mig walking towards the road and his bike, watching as he straddled the bike, gave a hard glare at his house, then started his bike up with a roar.

My brows rose as I saw him speed out of the little road we were both located on, and laughed when I heard his bike all the way to the highway.

My phone rang just as I moved back away from the window, and I smiled when I heard Lenore's voice.

"Hey! Wanna come hang with me so I won't be the only girl?" Lenore asked cheerily.

I thought about my life and how I never did anything.

How I would never meet another Mig if I didn't get myself out there, and I came to a decision.

I was going to have to get over my crush on Mig.

And I was going to have fun doing it.

"Sure," I said, walking to my bedroom to get dressed. "Where am I meeting you, and do I need to bring anything?"

I made a half-assed attempt to fluff up my hair, and in the end decided to put it up in a high pony tail, following it up with a swipe of mascara as I listened to Lenore give me directions.

"Where is this place?" I asked after she'd told me what turns I needed to take to get there.

"It's…shit. I gotta go. I'll see you there in ten, I forgot I was supposed to bring beer."

I shook my head as I reached for my tightest pair of jeans that I had, shimmying into them and wincing when I pinched my belly in my attempt to button them.

After three more tries, I got the button done and the zipper up before I threw on a plain black halter top, slipped my feet into a pair of flip flops, and started towards my front door.

I grabbed my purse, and armed the new alarm, being very sure that I got the numbers correct, before I backed out of the house, locked the door with the key and hurried to the street where I'd parked my car.

Although there was parking in the back of the house, I liked parking out front because it gave me more opportunities to see Mig.

And yes, I realize that I have an unhealthy obsession with the man.

But a girl can fantasize!

It was literally a hundred and fifteen out, and no matter how many years I'd been dealing with this humid Texas heat, I'd never get used to it.

I followed Lenore's directions to a T and found myself at a house that was about a hundred yards shy of the river.

The closer I got to the front door, the more nervous I became.

This didn't look like a place to drink. This looked like someone's house!

I pulled my phone out and called Lenore.

"Umm," I said once she answered. "Where the hell am I?"

"You're at The Uncertain Saints' clubhouse," Mig said from behind me.

I jumped and turned, and my heart started to pitter-patter.

This definitely wouldn't work well with my whole 'try to get over Mig' plan.

***

Mig

I don't really know what I expected out of this night.

Peace and quiet.

Time to chill and just be one with the world.

It was definitely supposed to be a much needed breather from my bitch of a wife.

What I didn't think I'd see was the one woman that never failed to make my heart beat faster.

The one that I just couldn't seem to stop thinking about.

And we were having an in-depth discussion with the whole fuckin' club about why I didn't like my wife.

"Why don't you divorce her? I don't understand why you put up with her if she did that to you," Annie asked with confusion.

She was about two beers in, and I liked her this way.

She was chatty instead of nervous, and I found that *this* Annie was also fun to watch.

Not that I didn't like her sober, but I liked how the alcohol loosened her up, and she didn't hesitate to say what was on her mind.

I was lucky to get more than two sentences out of her on a normal day.

Which was why I was talking about this subject instead of shutting it down.

I *wanted* to talk to her.

"That's because he has the morals of a damn preacher. His conscience won't allow him to drop her like she deserves," Peek offered from his position across the table. Peek was the president of our little motorcycle club, and a major pain in the ass sometimes.

Annie blinked.

"Why? I know she did something bad. You don't get off on treating women badly. Yet every single woman you meet, you're suspicious of," Annie said.

I did do that.

But I couldn't help it.

"When my father started to date after my mother and he split up, he'd bring every single one of his bitches home to meet me. And every one of them was nice as could be in front of my father, but the moment he left the room, they could care less about me.

"That continued for the rest of my childhood. Then I started dating, and women just kept proving to me over and over again how devious they are. I've yet to find one, besides the one I can't have, that aren't bitches," I told her.

Annie's eyebrows rose.

"You're not calling me a deceptive, manipulative bitch, are you?" She teased.

I gave her back an eyebrow raise in return.

"I said 'besides the one I can't have.' not being bitches. That's you," I told her.

She snorted. "I never said you couldn't have me."

My heart started to race.

"You know I can't," I said.

She shrugged.

"I guess I'll settle for being your only female friend then," she teased.

I snorted.

"You can come drink beer with us anytime you want," I invited, gesturing to the table of my friends.

Peek and his wife, Alison. Griffin and his woman, Lenore. Wolf and his kid, who was currently sleeping in his room. Ridley and Casten. Even Apple, the prospect, wasn't half bad.

We were a bunch of people that had become family out of necessity.

And I would trust each and every one of my brothers to have my back if I needed it.

And Annie was easily becoming one of the few women in the world I would trust.

"I don't think I've ever actually heard why you and your wife got together. What's the big deal?" Lenore asked with confusion.

I was surprised Griffin hadn't shared.

It wasn't a secret.

It just pissed me off to think about.

So I didn't tell anyone if I didn't have to.

Which luckily wasn't often since my brothers were more than willing to tell it, like it was obvious that Wolf was ready to do.

"Jennifer came to one of our parties. We don't have many, so when we do open them up to the public, quite a few people show up," Wolf started. "This bitch must really have been jonesing for this party, because the moment she walked into the door, she locked her eyes on Mig."

"Now, anyone who's been around this town for a while knows that Mig isn't exactly the nicest one of us. He doesn't even pretend to be. So there she was, walking straight in and right up to Mig like they knew each other," Wolf continued. "And not one of us thought it was odd at the time. We went on about our business, drinking and having fun. Mig tried to ignore the woman and was doing spectacularly at it until a fight broke out among two young girls over who was going to play pool next."

"Okay… So, what happened then?" Annie asked while Wolf paused to take a sip of his beer.

"What happened next was cloudy for most of us. All we saw was Mig breaking up the fight, then going back to his table where he was talking to a couple local officers and drinking his beer," Griffin started. "The next thing we know, he's taking Jennifer to his bedroom and leaving the party. But who are we to block him from what he wants."

"Except…" Annie urged.

"Except for Mig waking up the next morning totally blank on what happened, with a headache from hell, and a sore cock," Ridley piped in.

Annie blinked, turning to me.

"You were drugged?" Her voice rose.

I nodded, the bile burning deep.

"Went to the doctor the next morning thinking I was dying. Turns out I had enough roofies in my system to knock out a two-ton rhino," I answered.

37

"And you think it was Jennifer?" Annie asked.

"I know it was Jennifer. Went searching for her the next day and found her brother who informed me just how vindictive his sister really is. Took me to her room in the apartment they shared, saw the fuckin pill bottle that the roofies came in. Took it to have it tested, then came back to confront Jennifer a week later where she told me her plan. Apparently, her mother had helped her come up with a plan to bag herself an 'heir' as a husband," I answered.

"You're an heir?" She asked.

Casten slid the bottle of vodka he'd been sharing with Ridley for the last half hour across the table.

It came to a stop in front of Annie, and she was looking at it in confusion.

"My dad owns Konn Vodka," I answered.

Her eyes widened.

"I think I have some of that in my cabinet right now," she answered, turning the bottle around.

"I think everyone does," Lenore answered, pulling the bottle to her and looking at the label.

"So what happened next?" Annie asked.

"Didn't hear from her again for eight weeks. Then she shows up at my work and tells me that she's pregnant," I answered.

"And you fucking married her?" Annie screeched.

I snorted.

"After I had a DNA test to make sure the kid was mine, yes."

Annie shook her head. "And I thought my ex-husband was bad."

I snorted. "Maybe we could compare notes about the shittiness of our spouses."

"He's not my spouse anymore. You're fucked, I'm not."

Ain't that the truth?

"We have a poll going to see when he breaks it off with her," Casten said, getting up and walking to the board at the back of the room and pulling it to the table.

I rolled my eyes at the men's guesses that were written down on the huge dry erase board that they'd bought specifically for my viewing pleasure.

Griffin's guess of a month had already passed seeing as we'd been married for six now.

The rest of the guesses spanned from an eight-month time period to two years.

And the way I left it with Jennifer tonight, I doubted that I'd be seeing eight months.

I'd gotten home from work early for once, but only because I'd needed to change my clothes before I went to the clubhouse.

And I'd found Jennifer on the couch talking to someone.

She'd freaked when I'd shown up, immediately hanging up the phone and looking at me like she'd seen a ghost.

I had a feeling if I took her phone away from her, I'd have seen a man on the receiving end of Jennifer's call.

Something I planned on researching tomorrow.

But that wasn't even the biggest problem.

Once Jennifer realized I was going out without her, she'd threatened to leave.

When I'd left anyway, I'd seen her staring at me like I'd committed a sin right in front of God himself.

"Can I get in on that?" Annie asked, tossing me a wink over her shoulder.

I wanted to wrap her up in my arms.

Instead, I shook my head and stared at the board as Ridley wrote down Annie's guess.

Seven months.

And for some reason, I had a feeling that she was about to pull out all the stops when it came to us.

And I was about to have a hell of a time resisting her.

Because when it came to Annie, I had no resistance.

The only thing keeping me from taking her as my own was Annie not pursuing *me*.

If she started to do that, then I'd be well and truly fucked.

Figuratively *and* literally.

The real test would be whether she acted like she was doing now when she didn't have two beers in her…and I found that I rather liked thinking about her pursuing me.

But that didn't negate the fact that I still had a wife.

CHAPTER 4

It's a proven fact that bearded men give better oral sex. Ten out of ten women agree.
-Annie's secret thoughts

Mig

The next morning turned out to be an exercise in patience.

"I'm not going to be there today. I have some papers to file," I told Griffin.

"Fine with me. But I'm not your boss. Why are you calling me?" Griffin asked. "And what kind of papers are you filing?"

I rolled my eyes.

"I'm calling you because I'm supposed to meet you in half an hour at the office to discuss the case. But I can't make it there until after lunch, if at all. I have some digging to do…then I'm going to need to go to the courthouse," I answered dryly.

"You're divorcing her, aren't you?" Griffin asked, relief evident in his voice. "Thank fuckin' Christ."

"I'll catch up with you later in the afternoon," I said, hanging up without giving an answer.

I was at my house, sans my wife.

My wife had woken up at six in the morning and had left before I'd gotten back from my morning run.

Granted, I didn't much care when she left.

But today I'd intended to follow her to see if she was actually going to work.

It was Sunday, after all.

Most people didn't go to the office, where they were a receptionist, on Sundays.

And even if they did, perchance, have to go into work on a Sunday, it wouldn't be at a little past six thirty in the morning.

I usually ran for an hour, and I'd left the house at five twenty.

I arrived home at six twenty to an empty house, pissed off that I'd decided to run early instead of later in the day like I'd told myself to do just because of this very reason.

So now I had to find her.

But first I had to find a car that wasn't so noticeable.

Lucky for me, I had a neighbor that had one.

I didn't even care that it was so early. She'd open the door for me no matter what time it was.

I just slipped a t-shirt on over my still wet chest, grabbed my cut from the chair that designated me as a member of the Uncertain Saints MC, and threw it on over my shirt as I walked out my front door.

I paused to lock the door to the house, thinking I'd need to find Jennifer an apartment this afternoon as well and hire some movers that could come out either today or tomorrow to box and move her shit out of the house.

As I made the mental list of things I needed to finish today, I walked across the space that separated my house from Annie's and went right up her front steps.

I knocked loudly, then bent over to pick a piece of paper off the front porch.

I want you back.

Four simple, little words that had the power to send rage coursing through my veins.

Here I was, fucking married, and I was getting pissed off that Annie's ex wanted her back.

What a head case I was.

"Ohh," a voice said from behind me.

I slowly stood up and handed her the note.

But her eyes were still focused on where my ass had been ten seconds before, which meant she got a good look at the erection that was starting to fill out the front of my pants simply from hearing the husky sound of her 'just woke up' voice.

Her face flushed, and I finally got my first good look at her without being 'all done up.'

Her hair was a mess of curls, all piled into a bun on top of her head.

Her face, free of makeup, had me wanting to see it every morning across the pillow from me.

She was wearing tight black shorts that barely covered her ass and a pink tank top that only accentuated the fact that she wasn't wearing a bra.

The sight of her unbound breasts had my mouth watering with the urge to suck them.

They were perky and luscious, even with their larger size.

I could make out the outline of her nipples through the thin fabric, and I had to clench my hands to keep from reaching out and tracing the pattern with my fingers.

To cover up the problem I was having with gathering the ability to speak, I thrust the note in her direction.

"I'm guessing this is from your husband?" I asked.

She glanced down at the paper like it was a snake ready to strike.

"You can toss it into the trash," she offered, opening the door wider for me to come in.

I passed by her, accidentally brushing my right arm against her breasts as I moved.

I swallowed, trying to get into her kitchen without making a complete fool of myself.

"Where'd you find it?" Annie asked as she moved into the kitchen behind me.

"Your front porch," I answered, letting the trash fall into the can before I turned around and pinned her to the spot with my gaze. "I want to borrow your car."

She lifted her brows at me.

"Why?" She asked in confusion. "Is there something wrong with your bike?"

I shook my head, surveying her kitchen.

She had a huge pile of mail along the back of the counter next to the back sliding door.

The other surfaces in the kitchen were spic and span.

"Nothing wrong with my bike," I answered. "I just need to borrow yours for a couple hours."

She crossed her arms and gave me the glare.

You know the one.

Every woman had it perfected before they even hit the age of eighteen.

The one that was supposed to make a man tremble in his boots.

With Jennifer, that move didn't work at all.

With Annie, though, it only made my primal instincts flare to life.

The urge to fuck the attitude right out of her was instinctive and nearly overwhelming.

"I want to follow Jennifer, but she knows my truck and bike. You drive that little hatchback, and about fifteen hundred people in the vicinity have that car," I finally answered.

She snorted.

"Was that so hard?" She asked, handing me the keys to her car. "But it's empty…like running on fumes empty, and I need to leave in about thirty minutes to meet someone."

"Who are you meeting?" I asked.

She walked to a table where a pile of what looked to be garage sale items sat.

A pillow. A black leather bag. A vase. And a huge rock.

"I'm selling some of my old stuff. I need to have a garage sale, but I'm a lazy person, so I'm not gonna do that. I'll just sell off a little but at a time," she answered, pointing to the stuff.

"And you're going to go meet where?" I asked.

"The mall parking lot," she answered just as quickly, walking into the back bedroom.

"That's not very safe," I said, walking to the living room and looking at the pictures on her walls and mantle as she dressed.

In the first picture she was sitting with her sister, a woman I'd seen from

45

afar since she'd moved in beside me.

The other two were, I guessed, her parents.

They were older versions of the girls, and they were smiling. The man with his arm around the sister. The woman with her arm around Annie.

A picture perfect family.

"I don't think it's unsafe. I'm meeting them all around eight this morning in the mall parking lot," she said from the other room.

The mall wasn't actually a 'mall.'

It was a store on the Uncertain/Jefferson border that was sort of a mini dollar store.

It had a little bit of everything, which was why the owners called it the mall even though it wasn't technically labeled as one.

It was also out in the middle of fuckin' nowhere, Texas…and not somewhere I'd want Annie meeting someone by herself.

"The mall is not a good place for you to be meeting. And if you're going to do it today, then I'm coming with you," I said, booking no room for an argument.

She didn't answer, which gave me more time to study her photos.

The other ones on the wall were of Annie and her friends, women I'd seen coming here to her house to visit quite a few times since she'd moved in as well.

The last photo my gaze caught on, however, was the one of Annie in a white dress that came all the way down to her ankles.

She was dressed all in white…her wedding dress…with her dad standing at her side looking down at her adoringly.

She was younger, of course, but she was still the same woman I saw every morning as I walked to my bike on the way to work.

The same woman who I'd dreamt about every night since she'd moved in next to me.

"I'm ready," Annie said from behind me.

I turned, giving one last longing look at the picture before turning to her.

"Cool, let me have your keys," I instructed.

She raised her head, but nonetheless dropped the keys into my palm.

"Be nice to my baby. She's on her last legs," Annie instructed.

I nodded. "Okay. I'll try."

In truth, I didn't think I'd have a problem being gentle with her.

We were on our way, twenty minutes later, with Annie in the passenger seat next to me.

"This has got to be the smallest car I've ever had the experience of sitting in," I grumbled, shifting the gears once again.

Annie laughed.

"Well, you're six foot three; what'd you expect?" She teased.

I turned onto the road that would take us to the mall and looked over at her.

She was even more beautiful in the morning sun.

The light from the sun shone into her hair, making it have a shimmery, fiery look to it.

She'd changed into a pair of jeans and a plain black t-shirt.

She put black boots on that resembled the female version of my own, an expensive pair that I wore nearly every day because they were safe to ride in.

Her hair was in a ponytail up high on her head.

And her hair was still just as messy as the moment she'd answered the door, and I found that I quite liked the look on her.

"I don't like that you're meeting out here," I muttered to myself.

However, Annie picked up on it the moment I spoke and started to look around with me.

"I really don't see what's wrong," she grumbled.

She wouldn't. She was a woman, after all.

"Shit," Annie said suddenly. "Pull in there and let me get a bag. They asked me to wrap it."

I thought that weird, but I didn't say anything as I pulled into the Dollar Store and watched as she hurried into the store, bought the first thing she could find close to the register, and immediately went to the checkout.

"Okay," Annie said, dropping into the seat as she tossed a smile my way.

I lifted my brows up at her.

"Tell me about selling your stuff online. What does the process entail?" I asked, backing up.

I couldn't see shit with her tiny ass mirrors.

So I rolled the window down, turned my head around and contorted my body into a weird angle so I didn't take anything out with her car.

My luck I would total it.

"I put the stuff I want to sell on a specific Facebook group geared towards garage sale items, and people comment whether they want it or not. Then we meet in a specified spot and complete the transaction," she informed me, pulling up her phone and scrolling through it.

She turned the phone to me when I reached a stop sign, and I read the post she'd made in *Uncertain Garage Sale Page, Buy, Sell or Trade*.

"Do you make any money doing this?" I asked, pulling out and speeding up to the required sixty miles an hour speed limit.

"A little bit. Mostly, I do it because I don't like clutter," she said.

I nodded.

I didn't like clutter, either.

And I really didn't like it now.

Jennifer was notorious for not cleaning up after herself.

How hard was it to put the coffee cup away that you used?

Even more, would it kill her to wash the fucker out in the sink?

"He's going to be in a blue car on the side of the building," Annie said.

"FYI, I still think this is a stupid idea."

Annie laughed. "Noted."

CHAPTER 5

It takes 200 muscles to fake an orgasm. One bearded man can save you a lot of trouble.
-E-card

Annie

"This isn't what I ordered, bitch. You said it was a Coach purse, not a…" he never had the chance to finish what he was saying.

Mig struck like a snake.

One second he was leaning against a tree talking on his phone, and the next he had the guy by the throat and he was throwing him across the small parking lot.

The guy hit the gravel with a hard thud and skidded.

The rocks on the ground underneath his body made soft tinkling noises as he moved over them, making me wince.

The man would have one hell of a road rash after that landing

"Don't fuckin' put your hand in her face. What the fuck are you thinking?" Mig snarled, standing over the man.

"Mig…" I started, but he held his hand up to stop me from continuing.

"I'm not some fuckin' man that'll stop just because you want me to. I'm me, and me is what you get. Right now, you'll let me handle this little piece of shit," Mig said with a deadly quiet tone.

I nodded, backing up to sit on the bench at the side of the store, to watch the scene before me unfold.

"Now, how's about you tell me what made you so upset that you'd get into a woman's face like that." Mig ordered the man at his feet.

"She didn't give me what I ordered. Tried to fuck me over," the man said petulantly.

Mig's head tilted. "You didn't comment on her post on that online garage sale site?"

The man nodded.

"And what'd you expect to get? She explained to me on the way here how it all worked," Mig growled.

"I ordered a Coach purse, wrapped. She had it in her post that she'd wrap it," the man screamed.

"I did wrap it!" I screamed right back, pointing to the pile of tissue paper and torn bag I'd purchased on the way here.

"You lying bitch! I just gave you a hundred and fifty dollars! You owe me two ounces!" The man spat.

Mig froze at the mention of 'two ounces' but I didn't.

I picked up the bag that he'd thrown on the floor.

"This weighs more like a pound. What the hell does two ounces have to do with anything?" I fumed.

But before I could hand the money that I'd just ripped out of my pocket over to the man, Mig stopped me in my tracks.

"Call Griffin and get him here," Mig ordered, handing me his phone.

I took it and opened it, then began searching through his contacts for Griffin.

I didn't dwell on the fact that I had to pass an Angel, Barbara, Brianne, Cathy, Caty, DeeDee , Diane, Dora and Giselle to get to Griffin, though.

Okay, maybe I did a little bit.

If the first seven letters in his phone book had seven women in it, how many did the rest of his phone hold?

Once I found Griffin's name, I hit call and held the phone to my ear as I watched Mig continue to question the man.

"Yeah?" A rough male voice grated from the other end of the line.

"Umm," I hesitated. "This is Annie. Mig asked me to call you and ask you to please come out here."

Griffin snorted. "I'm sure he asked real nice, exactly like that, too," Griffin laughed. "Where are you?"

"The mall," I answered.

"The actual mall in Marshall or the mall in between Jefferson and Uncertain?" Griffin clarified.

"The one in between Jefferson and Uncertain," I answered quickly, flinching when Mig hauled the man up by his shirt and shook him. "And you might want to hurry before Mig goes all hardcore on this man."

"Be there in fifteen, maybe less," Griffin rang off, and I shoved the phone into my back pocket.

"He said he'd be here in fifteen minutes," I answered, deciding to leave off the 'maybe less.'

Mig didn't acknowledge me, and I wondered idly whether I should call the police or not.

I decided against it, however, when Mig started to punch the man.

I bit my lip and watched.

I was ashamed to admit it, but the sight of Mig being so upset and bothered about me nearly being hurt was really turning me on.

I watched as the muscles in his arms bunched and released.

Mig's grip on the man's shirt loosened, but only long enough for Mig to put his entire hand across the man's neck and squeeze.

I don't know why I wasn't more worried than I was.

I knew Mig wouldn't hurt him too badly.

And he sure wouldn't kill him.

"I asked you to tell me what you meant," Mig ordered slowly.

The man started to cry.

"I was trying to buy drugs!" The man finally wailed. "Coke, man. I was trying to buy some fucking coke!"

I blinked.

He thought I was a drug dealer?

"Why would you think she was giving you drugs? She showed me the post. Nowhere in that post are drugs ever mentioned or even hinted about," Mig snarled, leaning close.

I wanted to laugh as the man started to cry.

I was such a bitch!

"She used the code! Wrapping it. *'Got it. Red tissue paper.'* She said that in her reply, man!"

I wanted to throw my hands up in exasperation.

Seriously?

I'd used the code back to him?

I'd been teasing about how I had to wrap it, never even realizing that I'd inadvertently set up a drug deal!

"I thought you weren't working today," Griffin said from behind us, making me squeak in surprise.

Mig looked up at Griffin and glared. "I haven't had the chance to do what I needed to do yet because of this little shit head."

Mig shook the man for emphasis.

"What's going on?" Griffin asked, making no move to stop Mig from hitting the man one more time.

"Motherfucker tried to hit Annie when his supposed drug deal went south. Annie had no clue she was agreeing to deliver drugs. Seems the garage sale site she uses sets up code words in the posts to place their order and set up the deal. They settle on a meeting place, and the seller uses the code phrase in the reply," Mig answered, standing up.

When the man tried to stand up as well, Mig fixed him with a stare.

"Stay where you are."

The man flopped back onto the ground, and I would've laughed had this situation not been scary.

What would've happened if I had been by myself like I'd originally intended?

Would I be dead?

CHAPTER 6

I used my manners today. Bitch, please is adequate, right?
-Annie's secret thoughts

Annie

If you'd have asked me two weeks ago what I would be doing today, it would've never been what I was doing.

"Are you sure this is legal?" I asked once more.

Mig glared at me.

"Yes," he insisted. "It's my car!"

"Actually, it's your wife's car," I informed him. "And what are you hoping to accomplish by having me move it?"

"I'm hoping that she'll try to call someone," he informed me, shutting the door on my retort.

I moved his wife's car behind the building, parked it in the back behind a dumpster and got out.

I headed back to my car, while Mig dutifully followed behind me the entire way.

"You know the phrase *stealing from a baby?*" I asked him as I dropped into the passenger side of my car.

My eyes went down to the junk in the floorboard.

Since I never sat on this side of the car, I never realized just how dirty it was.

It needed a wash…bad.

"Yeah, why?" He asked, whipping the car around so fast that my head spun.

"Mig!" I cried out, grasping the 'oh shit', or 'OS', handle and holding on for dear life.

Mig laughed.

I wanted to punch him.

"That's what it feels like I just did. Stealing a pregnant woman's car," I admitted to him.

He pulled up beside the store, just to the side of where Jennifer's car had been parked, and got out.

I followed suit, and we leaned against the hood as we watched the front doors.

"It's my car. And I won't let her walk home. She'll find a ride, and if I'm right, she'll find one with someone that's not me," he informed me.

I blinked.

"What makes you think it won't be you she calls?" I asked.

He shrugged. "Jennifer never calls me. Never. She barely talks to me unless it's to bitch about something…or someone."

I still didn't know what to think about all that was Jennifer.

She always had a perpetual scowl on her face.

She's never once waved hello the few times we'd seen each other

She didn't speak to me. Didn't ever help Mig out in the yard.

And with Mig's explanation about what had really happened to bring the two of them together, it all seemed to make a sick sort of sense.

Why I never saw them hug. Why she watched him leave every day with a glare on her face.

Why I'd never seen them be affectionate to each other. Why I'd never seen them hug or kiss. Often, I could hear them both screaming at each other.

Mig's phone chimed for the fourth time in less than ten minutes, and I looked at him with a questioning gaze.

"Need to leave?" I asked hopefully.

He shook his head, pulling his phone out, tapping out a few words, then replacing it.

"No. It's Griffin giving me updates on Carl Copeland," he said. "He's got quite a bit of interesting information."

I nodded.

Carl Copeland, as I'd later learned was his name, was a small time boy just looking for his next fix.

But, apparently, both Griffin and Mig had thought there was more to the story, so he was escorted by Griffin to their office where he would continue asking him questions, hoping to get more information out of him than he originally had.

"And?" I asked, bored out of my mind.

Who knew a stakeout would be so boring?

"Got a few names we need to track down. Griffin's sending them to the computer people to get dossiers on them," Mig explained. "You need to be careful, though."

I blinked. "What? Why?"

He raised a brow at me that I saw over the top of his sunglasses.

"You nearly got yourself caught up in a botched drug deal, and everyone else saw the message you sent to that man. You may have deleted it, but that shit always comes back to bite you in the ass," he explained.

"You think someone else is going to contact me about getting drugs?" I asked in alarm.

Mig shrugged. "Maybe, maybe not."

Oh, great. Now I was freaking out.

"What do I do if I get contacted about that?" I asked worriedly. "What if they show up at my shop?"

Mig looked at me, studying me so long that I worried I asked a stupid question.

"Do you have an alarm at your shop?" He asked.

I shook my head.

"No. There's nothing really in it to steal. While I'm doing massages, I lock the door. The only thing they could get to if they broke in is about two hundred bottles of shampoo, conditioner, mousse and lotion," I answered.

He nodded, turning back to the door when someone came outside.

My breath caught in my throat when I saw Jennifer standing there with a huge bag in her hand.

She looked around the parking lot, her face showing her confusion as she turned in a slow circle.

Her arms crossed over her chest, her large bag slammed against her stomach, and Mig growled.

My breath caught as I watched Mig watch her.

He may not love Jennifer, but he did love their baby.

And when Jennifer stomped to a bench on the side of the store, fell heavily into it, then pulled out her phone, I hoped beyond hope that Mig's phone would ring.

Instead, I waited with bated breath as she called someone else, spoke for a few long minutes with wild hand gestures, then dropped the phone back into her purse.

She crossed her arms over her stomach angrily and glared at the parking spot where her car had been sitting.

Mig slowly let out a breath at my side, and I turned to him once again.

"Do you want your baby?" I asked carefully.

He nodded.

"Yeah."

Simple as that.

No more, no less.

That was totally Mig.

Would he change his mind about Jennifer when she gave birth to their child?

Children changed everything, absolutely everything.

My parents like to talk all the time about how they had grand plans on traveling the world.

Then I was born, and all their plans were derailed…not that they were that upset about it.

I was supposedly the 'best thing that ever happened to them.'

Although, I'd heard my mother say the same thing to my sister, so I knew she was lying to one of us.

But children were used as pawns in divorce all the time.

Would this child be?

I hoped not.

The child deserved to have two parents who could at least be cordial to one another.

And I hoped beyond hope that the story of the baby's conception forever stayed a secret.

We waited for long minutes, and just when I was about to suggest we go over there, Mig leaned forward.

"Bingo," he growled.

I blinked, studying the parking lot.

That was when I saw the white Mercedes.

Mig started to repeat letters and numbers to himself as he pulled out his phone, then he typed it in before shoving it back into his pocket.

I wondered what those letters had meant until I saw Jennifer round the car and open the passenger door.

And the brief glance we got of the driver had my stomach plummeting.

"I know him!" I said, thinking back to the client that I saw every Tuesday and Friday. "I give him massages twice a week after he plays a few rounds of golf at the country club just outside of town."

Mig growled.

"What's his name?" He asked.

I closed my eyes and thought of the name that was just on the tip of my tongue.

"Larry...Leonel...no...Liam!" I said excitedly. "His name is Liam Cornell."

"What's he do?" Mig asked, turning to me once the car that was picking

Jennifer up pulled out into traffic.

I shook my head. "I don't know. I only massage him twice a week. During those times, he has his ear phones in, and I barely say a word to him the entire time."

Mig blinked.

"Is that your way with every male client?" He asked.

I nodded. "Every female client as well. I try to stay out of their business while I'm massaging, since it's such a personal experience. As for doing hair, that's when I'll know my clients better."

Mig nodded. "What times does he usually come?" He continued.

I pursed my lips. "Normally just after lunchtime. Around two or so. I'm guessing he comes straight from his weekly golf game because it's not often that I don't see him decked out in his golfing attire."

"That tomorrow?" He asked me.

I nodded. "It's a first come, first serve system. We don't make appointments, so I just assume he's coming. But he hasn't missed one in three months."

Mig smiled. "Well, then I guess I'll see you at lunch tomorrow."

Lani Lynn Vale

CHAPTER 7

I hate being sexy, but I'm a bearded man. I can't help it.
-Mig to Annie

Mig

"This better not get me into trouble," she muttered to the man currently sitting on the counter in front of me.

Griffin shrugged, and the other man occupying her barber chair spun around for the fourth time.

Ridley stopped to study himself in the mirror.

"Do you think I could use a cut?" He asked the group as a whole, fingering his shaggy hair.

Nobody said anything.

Ridley was what you would call 'sensitive' about his hair.

Although it wasn't overly styled, his blonde hair always fell a certain way.

It never went over an inch and a half in length, and rarely ever did I see it a mess.

We all secretly thought he had some kind of issue with his hair.

Some sort of fetish having to do with his locks, but none of us ever asked.

We were all in the front of Annie's store, *Uncertain Salon and Massage*.

Griffin was sitting next to his wife on top of the counter next to the register.

Ridley occupied the lone barber chair, and I was sitting next to Annie on the couch.

We weren't touching, but we were close.

I was, however, very aware of her body.

Aware of how her body heat, however slight it was, felt like it was burning me.

I wanted to run my hand up the side slit of her skirt to see what kind of panties she had on underneath the frilly, gauzy slip of fabric.

She was wearing a hot pink halter top that barely confined her beautiful breasts, and to top it all off, she was shoeless.

Her toes were painted a hot pink, and I wanted nothing more than to lick her from the tips of those toes all the way up to her lips.

My hand came down on the chair between us touching the toes in question.

She didn't move, and neither did I.

Although the touch was innocent, I wondered if she could feel the promise.

It may only be her feet right now, but after I was officially divorced, which hopefully would only take a couple more days since it paid to know people in high places, she would be mine.

It may make me sound like a complete jack wad, but I couldn't help it.

I'd wanted Annie since she'd moved in next to me. And now that I'd finally allowed myself to complete the final papers for filing an annulment between Jennifer and me, I knew things were about to change between us.

When my parents had divorced, I'd made a promise to myself, that if a child was ever involved, I would go out of my way to make things work between the mother and me.

I would never put my child in the middle.

And over the last six months, I'd tried.

Oh, how I'd tried.

But this was no way to live.

This would never work for us.

Jennifer had wronged me greatly, and I'd allowed it.

There was no way I could build a relationship with her after what she did to me

Annie had helped me see that just by asking a few innocent questions.

Questions that my club brothers asked me on a daily basis.

But finally listening to it from someone who was in my life but who hadn't been around during that time had been an eye-opening experience had definitely hammered home how stupid I was being.

And I was about to be free for the first time in *long* months.

"This isn't going to get you in trouble, Annie," I said with patience. "It's not like I'm going to talk to him while he's getting a massage."

I was lying.

That *was* what I was planning to do.

She didn't need to know that, though.

Being naked made a person feel a certain vulnerability, and I wanted to get this over with quickly and with as little bloodshed as possible.

"Well, he's here. I'm going next door with Lenore. Let me know when the fire's out," Annie said, jumping out of her seat.

Then she was gone, disappearing out the back entrance with Lenore in a little less than two point five seconds.

"She looks a little nervous," Griffin observed dryly.

I flipped him off and said, "Get gone, boys. I'll let you know what transpires."

Griffin and Ridley snorted.

"We'll be in the break room. Yell if you need us," Ridley said just before he disappeared into the small room off to the side of the salon.

According to Annie, Liam Cornell would enter into the building and go straight to the back room.

Usually around this time, Annie was grabbing her supplies she'd need for the massage.

Liam Cornell would go into the room on his own, after calling out a hello to get ready for the massage.

So I didn't confront him in the lobby.

I might have confronted him while he was naked.

Ok, I did. There was no might about it.

I waited until he'd gone as far as to lay on the table, face down.

I entered the room like I owned the place, ignored Cornell's call of greeting and immediately placed my hands viciously on Cornell's neck.

"I'm going to ask you one time and one time only. Are you fucking my wife?" I asked calmly.

Cornell stiffened under my hands, and I let him move when he put his arms onto the table and pushed up.

I stepped back, waiting to see what he'd do, and I wasn't disappointed.

"And what if I am fucking your wife, Mr. Konn? What are you going to do about it?" He asked. "Furthermore, are you even sure that the baby she's carrying is yours?"

I narrowed my eyes. "I'm not that stupid. I know the kid's mine."

"Do you? Are you sure she didn't fuck someone at the hospital to switch the results?" He countered cruelly.

The doubts started to swirl.

She'd done that to me.

Fucked me over.

Who's to say she didn't do the same thing by blackmailing someone else?

"I see my words hit home," Cornell said silkily. "And let me tell you this," he said, moving closer. "I fuck her every night since you're not there… right in your bed."

Everything degraded from there.

My fist swung out and connected with his face.

There was a satisfying crack as my fist connected with his jaw.

Pain exploded in my hand as bone met bone, but I didn't stop.

I hit him with a left. Right. Left.

Over and over again I hit him.

He, of course, tried to hit back.

But it didn't work.

I was too quick.

I had skills he could never even imagine.

I'd grown up fighting.

I'd had to fight in order to survive.

My father may have been a Vodka billionaire, but he'd made me earn every single penny he gave me.

By fighting.

And to a kid of ten years old, I hadn't known any different.

My mother never understood why I'd become the way I had.

Never understood why, after spending every summer at my father's after their divorce, I was a different kid each time I came back to her.

And to this day, she still didn't know just what my father made me do.

I understood it now, though.

Understood that my father was trying to prepare me for life.

I took no satisfaction in the way I effortlessly took Cornell down until he was panting and barely able to lift his head.

"The kid's mine. My wife, however, you can have if she wants you," I said, moving away from him. "Get the fuck out of here and don't come back."

I had to admit, I wasn't happy with the way I'd reacted to him.

And by the smile he gave me as he shuffled out the door with his clothes in his arms, I knew that wouldn't be the last time I saw him.

I just hoped that he didn't do anything to Jennifer.

However, never once did it occur to me that it shouldn't have been Jennifer I should worry about.

***

"You want me to leave?" Jennifer asked with fat tears running down her face.

I shook my head.

"No, you don't have to leave. But I want you actively trying to look for a place of your own," I answered. "Close by so we don't have to fight over our kid."

She closed her eyes and looked down.

"Why?" She asked.

I narrowed my eyes.

"How could you even ask that? After everything you've done, you have the nerve to ask me why?" I asked with disbelief.

She seemed to slump in on herself further.

"I'm not sleeping with him," she said stubbornly.

I narrowed my eyes at her.

"Then please, enlighten me," I growled.

She looked away, clutching her hands to her stomach in a protective gesture.

I looked up.

"The annulment will be filed at the court house by the end of the business day tomorrow. I'm giving you ten grand to get you on your feet. There's also going to be more papers coming for you, telling you the visitation schedule as well as the custody arrangements for the baby. We share custody, fifty-fifty. I get all major holidays except for Thanksgiving and New Years," I informed her.

She looked up at me, tears glimmering in her eyes and down her cheeks.

And I wasn't effected in the least.

"Where are you going?" She asked as I turned to leave.

I swiveled back to her.

"You've got no right to know that anymore. Move your shit to the second bedroom."

With that, I left.

And didn't look back.

CHAPTER 8

Bearded men make better lovers. They also make prettier babies.
It's a proven fact that was established at the beginning of time.
-Mig to Annie

Annie

Two weeks later

I was almost giddy as I hurried out of the backdoor of my store.

It was three o'clock, and I had Mig coming over later so I could cook
him some homemade enchiladas—*my mother's secret recipe.*

His annulment was final yesterday - yes, he apparently knew some
people - and he hadn't made it a secret that he was going to pursue a
relationship with me.

And I made it known that I would reciprocate.

I'd wanted him for a long, *long* time.

There was no way I was going to pass up this opportunity.

And I didn't care that his ex was still living with him.

In fact, I thought it was actually nice on his part.

If I'd found out that my ex had been cheating on me, he would've been
gone before he could finish saying, 'I'm sorry.'

Hell, my ex *had* been cheating on me, but it hadn't been a secret.

I'd let it happen time after time, not caring in the least.

The only thing my ex offered me was stability, and after I was able to save up enough cash, I'd filed for divorce.

But never once, in all my years, had I felt so many butterflies in my belly at the idea of seeing Ross.

But with Mig, I felt like those butterflies could burst right out of my belly and take flight.

Even the idea of only spending some time with him had me bouncing on the balls of my feet.

The door to the office slammed shut behind me, and I turned to lock the door.

I never even saw the blow coming.

One second I was fitting the key into the hole of the lock, and the next my brain was exploding in agony.

**

Mig

"So," Griffin called from his half of the office. "Have you fucked her yet?"

I held up the phone from underneath my ear and pointed it at him.

He started to laugh.

I was dawdling.

I'd completed the final papers for the annulment two weeks ago.

It was official yesterday.

I was now a free man, but I hadn't made Jennifer leave.

We were living exactly as we had been…but I couldn't find the nerve to tell her it was time to go.

I'd told her all about finding out about her affair.

She wasn't even sorry.

Hell, *I* wasn't sorry.

That didn't make it any easier to kick a pregnant woman carrying my child out of the house she'd been living in.

I felt nothing for Jennifer. Absolutely nothing.

I felt for the child, though.

I didn't want my child to suffer because I kicked his or her mother out of the house.

And I was being a coward.

I didn't know how to tell Annie I was going to let Jennifer stay as long as she needed to.

Annie, I knew, would be fine with me letting her stay.

What she wouldn't be fine with was letting me fuck her while my ex still lived in my home.

So I had a dilemma.

Griffin made a wide eyed look when he saw I was on the phone before turning back around to his desk to finish a report.

I rolled my eyes and went back to the conversation I was having with my boss.

"One of the men we brought in yesterday swears that the drugs came from your way. So I want you to be aware that you may have a new supplier in town now that you took out the kid's source," my boss, Drew Logan, explained.

A couple of months ago, Griffin and I had lucked out and seized a huge drug shipment all because we'd needed a ride back up the river when the fuel pump in our boat had gone out.

It'd all been very innocent. We had approached a man getting his boat ready to go out on the river but the man had fled, and we did what we did best, we gave chase.

The man had started throwing out things from his pockets, which Griffin had collected as we ran, and we assumed were drugs.

Since he was trying to disappear into the thick of the woods, I'd continued the chase while Griffin had called in a K-9.

Ridley had arrived while I'd apprehended the subject, and Ridley had discovered nearly a thousand pounds of marijuana in his boat.

"Did you get the report on the Coach Purse Kid?" I asked.

"Mmm-hmm. Good work. I'd be interested to know if anything else comes out of that," Logan said.

I agreed.

Although we hadn't had any more instances where we found anyone else trying to buy and sell drugs that way.

That, or maybe they were changing the code words or something.

There was no fuckin' telling.

"Alright," I said, standing up. "I need to go with Griffin to meet with an informant. I'll ask him if he thinks a new supplier is in town."

"Good. Check in tomorrow with what you find out," Logan said, then hung up.

"What was that about?" Griffin asked once I looked up at him.

I went to the water cooler in between his desk and mine and filled up a glass of water before I answered.

"Long thinks a new supplier is in town because one of the busts the boys in the office did last night said they got 'em from the river," I answered.

Griffin looked at me in disgust.

"What the fuck ever happened to transporting actual goods down the rivers instead of fuckin' drugs and guns? This is a fuckin' never-ending nightmare," Griffin grimaced.

I agreed.

And I would've commented, but Ridley burst through the doors like his ass was on fire.

"What the fuck?" I asked him.

Ridley's eyes turned to me.

"Annie was found unconscious about twenty minutes ago outside of her salon. She was taken to the hospital with a suspected brain injury caused by a blow to the head," Ridley said without preamble.

My stomach clenched, and I lurched out of my seat.

"Which hospital?" I asked, jerking my phone and keys off the desk and shoving them into my pocket.

Ridley gestured to his cruiser.

"I'll take you."

I didn't bother to argue. I just got in and rode, all the while trying not to freak out over my fuck up.

***

"She suffered some major trauma to her right temporal lobe from where the piece of wood struck her across the side of the head," Dr. Mack gestured to his face. "I can't tell you now what kind of effect that's had on her since there's so much swelling. Only time will tell."

I watched as the doctor explained all that was wrong with Annie to the people who I guessed were her parents and sister.

77

I was further back, listening in because that was the only way I'd hear exactly what was wrong with her.

Since I wasn't family, I technically wasn't allowed to be in her room at this point, but I was beyond caring.

Slipping away just as silently as I came, I made my way to her room, then slipped inside without anyone the wiser.

My heart sank as I saw Annie laying on that bed.

Her head was wrapped in white gauze, and what little I could see of her face and eyes were also bruised.

Every last bit of it.

There wasn't any unbruised skin on her entire face.

My hands raised, and I grabbed onto my head, trying to breathe through the pain that was ripping through my chest.

I closed my eyes, opening them once I thought I had enough control to get closer to her.

And that's when my eyes lit on the note.

I'd been curious when the doctor explained about it while he was telling her parents what had happened, asking about the significance of the note.

The note that Annie had refused to give up—the whole time they were working on her in the ER—was in a baggie next to her bed.

Once she'd been sedated she'd finally loosened her grip enough for the doctor to remove it.

It was in a plastic bag with the rest of her belongings, but I could read it clearly.

Before, you were just a passing fancy. A way to keep my ear to the ground.

Now, I'm watching you.

I don't like being threatened.

Even more, I don't like people I trust throwing me under the bus.

Your wife will be next if you pursue this. Be thankful that I didn't kill the bitch. Better watch yourself and yours.

I'm coming.

And I won't stop until I've taken everything you have ever loved.

I wanted to vomit.

It wasn't signed, but I knew who it was from.

Liam Cornell.

Annie had been bashed over the head with a fuckin' two by four all because I wanted to approach the fucker I thought was fucking my wife.

I'd done this.

"Mig," Annie's raspy voice called.

I turned to her quickly, seeing one of her eyes just barely open.

I leaned down until she could see my face, then grabbed her hand that was resting on top of the blankets.

"Hey, baby."

Annie smiled slightly.

"It'll be okay," she promised.

I wanted to cry.

Was it acceptable for a thirty-four-year-old man to cry? Because, right then, I wanted to.

Here I was, responsible for this happening to her, and she was trying to comfort me.

God, what had I done?

She'd been by me all this time.

I'd wasted so much time trying to make my life with Jennifer bearable, even though I wanted nothing more than to be with the woman next door.

I'd given it six months.

I even considered that I might be able to get over Jennifer's manipulation, for the sake of our child, a child I had a part in creating, willingly or not.

This child had no control over the circumstances of it's conception

They had no control over anything.

They were defenseless human beings that deserved to be protected.

And the more I listened to my friends, recalling all of the bad things that I'd experienced over the last six months, I knew that I would never be able to offer my child even resembling a loving, stable home with Jennifer in the picture.

My kid didn't need to know how much I despised Jennifer, but it would be impossible to conceal if I had to see her and deal with her shit on a daily basis.

But right then, with Annie's hand in mine, and her bruised puffy face staring back at me with understanding in her eyes, I realized that I couldn't do *this*.

I couldn't bring Annie into my life…not when I led a life that wasn't for the faint of heart.

I'd nearly gotten her killed with my need to have the element of surprise when I approached the bastard.

Something I'd done at Annie's expense.

Annie, who was such a beautiful, strong, caring woman.

Annie who'd helped me realize that I couldn't live with Jennifer for the rest of my life.

Annie who deserved much better than me.

She deserved a home with two point five kids. A husband that worked nine to five.

And I wasn't that.

I'd never work nine to five.

I hadn't wanted kids at all, but life didn't ask me what I wanted.

But I sure as fuck could make sure that I didn't bring this shit to Annie's front door anymore.

That, I had the power to do, and from this moment on, I would stay away from her.

Lani Lynn Vale

CHAPTER 9

Dildo: the original selfie stick.
-Uncertain Pleasures T-shirt

Annie

"Stubborn, pig-headed, heart-breaking, man," I muttered to myself as I walked into the back of my store.

I glared at the new lock, as well as the brand new alarm that'd appeared as if by magic.

I knew it was Mig, though.

Even though I hadn't seen him—not once—in a month, I knew without a shadow of a doubt that he was responsible.

Hell, he wasn't even living in his house, either.

His ex-wife was, though.

And I felt awkward as hell living in my house, so I'd put it on the market.

I'd also secretly hoped it would bring Mig out of the woodwork, but it hadn't worked.

Now I was back in my store's apartment much to, what I guessed was, Mig's chagrin.

Hence why I now had an alarm system, what I guessed to be a high tech security camera system, as well as a biker bodyguard that never introduced himself.

After talking with Lenore, though, I realized that the biker bodyguard was a 'prospect' or someone trying to get into the club.

I hadn't realized the Uncertain Saints were even looking for someone to add to their club, but I learned new things every day.

Kind of like Lenore being Griffin's 'old lady.'

I hadn't even realized there were such things as old ladies.

But after being informed by Lenore that old ladies were like the wives of the biker world, I realized that I really, really wanted to be one.

I just had to figure out where Mig was first.

Which was where I was going now.

According to Lenore, my partner in crime, Griffin and Mig worked in the same building.

And I had a legitimate reason to be there and ask for Mig's help.

I was rethinking my decision to go two minutes later as I drove down the road to the office Lenore had given me directions to this morning as I'd done her hair.

It didn't look like a DEA or Texas Ranger headquarters.

Not that I really had anything to go by.

In fact, I sat studying it so long that I didn't realize there was someone at the front of my car until they tapped on the hood.

I jumped, turning to find a glaring Mig at the front of my car.

And he did *not* look happy to see me.

Gathering what little courage I had, I got out of the car slowly, very aware of my head.

I still got head rushes when I went from sitting to standing quickly.

Then my head would start hurting for hours.

So I learned the hard way to do it slow, or else.

"Hey," I whispered.

I also learned that if I talked too loudly, that it seemed to jar something in my brain, making my head hurt.

Then again, loud noises, sudden movements, and chewing made my head hurt...it didn't take much.

His eyes narrowed on me, studying me from the tips of my toes to the top of my head.

"What are you doing here?" He rasped.

God, his voice!

It made shivers run down my spine, and my toes curl.

"I have something to show you...and run by you," I said.

And I did.

I never realized just why my husband had tried to break into my house that night a month and a half ago.

It wasn't until I moved my things back into my store that I realized the coincidences.

I walked around the car, passing right by him to get to my right back passenger seat.

I didn't question why I chose to go the front way that took me by him instead of around the back that was faster.

I could've sworn that he'd growled as I made my way past him.

But he didn't say a word, and neither did I.

Instead, I reached in for a huge box of junk I'd managed to pick up without breaking my head, and turned.

I froze when I saw how close Mig was to me.

He had to be standing only inches away from me, and the only thing separating us was the box in my hands.

"What is it?" He rumbled.

Then I was divested of my box, and he was walking across the street without another word.

I followed behind him, going at a much slower pace than him.

I hadn't been able to work out since I'd been hurt.

Yet again, the moment blood started to really work through my body, and my heart rate started to rise, a headache would be soon to follow.

But, it turns out, watching Mig's ass in his tight jeans made my blood pressure rise…and wouldn't you know it, a headache started to thud dully behind my eyes.

Well, that sucked!

I slowed down even more, allowing a large distance to separate the two of us, hoping that if I slowed down my head wouldn't get into the full blown kill-me-now range.

And surprisingly, it worked.

Mig's scowl as he held the door open for me had me rethinking the decision, though.

"What's wrong?" He asked once I reached his side.

I gently shook my head from side to side.

"Headache. Nothing I can't handle," I said, slowly passing between him and the door frame he so kindly held open for me.

He grunted as I passed by him, and my eyes nearly crossed as my front brushed against his.

The first person I saw when I entered the room was Griffin and his bright blue, knowing eyes.

I waved, and he winked, returning to his phone conversation without even a hello.

Mig brushed past me and said, "Over here."

I followed him to the desk and stopped just to the side of his chair.

He set the box down on the desk, and I took the time to look around the room.

It was pretty bare.

There were two desks with mounds of paperwork on each.

Two chairs behind each desk.

A bulletin board on the far wall, a water dispenser in the corner near the front door, and a dart board splitting the two halves of the room in the very front.

"What do you have that you want me to look at?" Mig rumbled.

I blinked, returning my gaze to him.

My mouth watered as I took in his face.

The longer than usual dark hair that was covering his head.

His gray eyes studied my face, first going to my right side where the piece of wood had connected with my head.

Then to my eyes which still showed a large amount of bruising, then down to take in my body.

I'd lost some weight, which he was obviously noticing.

I couldn't say I was bothered by it, though.

The one good thing that came out of all of this was being able to fit into my skinny jeans once again.

"Well?" He asked a little loudly, causing me to jump.

"Oh," I said, reaching to the box and opening the flaps. "I just saw these today and, at first, I couldn't figure out just what was bothering me, but the more I studied them, the easier it became to see."

I laid out each of my purses along the top of his desk until all six of them were in plain view.

My belly was a mass of fluttering butterflies as I looked at him.

"So you have a purse collection," he muttered.

I nodded.

"I used to, yes," I conceded.

His eyes narrowed on my words.

"Talk," he ordered.

I held up my actual purse, then showed him the symbols.

"They're fakes," I told him, indicating the purses I'd laid on the desk.

He looked at me with raised brows.

"So?" He asked.

I narrowed my eyes at him.

"I didn't purchase fakes. I'm not sure when they were replaced with these, but I most certainly had real ones that I purchased at actual Coach Stores," I told him.

I could tell he still didn't get it.

"I think my ex-husband switched my purses with these so he could have the real ones," I explained.

A light dawned.

"You think he stole your purses, then started selling drugs in them?" He continued.

I nodded. "Yeah, that's what I think he did."

He studied the purses.

"I think the night he came in, he was actually looking to switch out my purse," I indicated the one I was using. "With a fake one."

He nodded.

"I remember he had another bag in the large backpack he was carrying on him, but we deemed it not yours since yours was in his hands," Mig observed.

"I'm not really sure where my other purses are, but I think I can find that out through Ross," I said.

Mig nodded.

"You're not going to be in this at all. I'll take care of it. I don't want you to approach Autrey at all," he ordered.

I held up my hands.

"I won't, I promise," I lied.

He seemed to know I was lying, too.

But if that was the only way to get him to stop being so standoffish, I'd confront Ross a million times and still accept the sacrifice as worth it.

When he didn't reply, I stood up, repacking my box.

He stilled my hands when I went to take the purses.

"Leave them."

I left them, picking up my actual purse and making my way to the door.

"Thanks," I said.

But before I could push all the way through the front door, he stopped me by grabbing a hold of the bar that spanned the width of the door.

I turned just my head to look at him and caught him staring right at me.

His eyes were on my lips, and the moment I went to lift my hand and place it on his cheek, he jerked back like I was waving a gun in his face.

"Don't do anything stupid," Mig said, releasing the door.

I turned around and glared at the ass.

How could I think I was in love with him?

Then he opened the door for me and I walked out the door.

I got into my car, put it into drive and then started to leave.

But the last thing I saw was Mig watching me drive away.

And I knew with one look that he didn't want me to go.

Knew it like I knew I'd draw another breath.

He wanted me, but he also wanted to protect me from what he thought was his dangerous life.

But his excuse had proven for naught today as I gave him my theory on just why I was somehow involved in the middle of a drug deal. Plus, I knew a drug dealer… my ex-husband.

What he failed to recognize was that I'd found it on my own.

Sure, his situations only added to mine, but it wasn't like I was going into this life without my eyes wide open.

And I was about to prove to him just who and what I could be…and what kind of situations I could get in.

I smiled.

Oh, this would be fun!

Lani Lynn Vale

CHAPTER 10

*I'm not a violent person unless you wake me up early. Even a
minute early. Ever do that again, and I'll cut you.*
-Text from Tasha to Annie

Mig

I was fairly positive that women didn't have nine lives like cats did.

In fact, their one wasn't even worth all that much.

"You've got to be fucking kidding me?" I growled, pinching the bridge
of my nose with two fingers. "Can you get her out?"

"No. I've tried about ten times now. Every time I tell her it's time to go,
she takes another shot," our newest prospect, Apple Drew, explained.

"Fuck," I growled, getting up from my computer chair. "I'll be there as
soon as I can. Ten minutes or less."

"Got it. But Mig," Apple hesitated. "Hurry."

I didn't bother to change.

I knew the moment I went into that bar that shit would start to fly…and I
had a feeling that Annie knew it, too.

There were about two areas in a fifty-mile radius of Uncertain and the
surrounding towns that The Uncertain Saints weren't welcome, and The
Hail House was one of them.

It was located in Jefferson, Texas.

The bar and grill was opened about twenty years ago and was established well before the Uncertain Saints were formed.

That's why we never made a huge deal about the crew that ran out of The Hail House, a team of auto recovery agents who were mostly motorcycle riders.

Although they weren't technically a MC, they were territorial.

They didn't like to start fights, but they would finish them.

And I knew, beyond a shadow of a doubt, that Annie had heard about them somewhere.

Knew that I wouldn't let her stay.

Not because they were dangerous to her physical body, but because they—other than the owner of Hail Auto Recovery—would be dangerous to her heart.

I was secure enough in myself to admit that they were all good looking.

And Annie seemed to be drawn to the bad boy type.

Although she probably didn't know exactly what she was getting into, she had to know that I'd come for her.

Knowing it was about to get ugly, I called up the boys.

I started with Ridley, since I knew he would be closest seeing as he was a sheriff's deputy out of Jefferson.

"Yeah?" Ridley answered with a slight hint of annoyance.

"Annie's at Hail House," I told him.

"Goddammit, this is not what I need right now. I'll be by there as soon as I can, but I've got my hands full at the mall right now...*motherfucking son of a bitch!*"

A scuffle ensued, and I knew Ridley was really in a predicament if he couldn't even speak.

Ridley was a big guy, over six foot two and two hundred fifty pounds, he could easily fit the description of a giant.

Ridley's grunt of pain had me running to my bike.

Although I wanted to go to Annie, I knew she would be safe.

Ridley, however, wouldn't be if the sounds coming from over the line were anything to go by.

Before I got onto my bike, I called one last person who I knew would round up the rest of the boys.

Our president, Peek.

"Yeah?" He growled.

I could hear the whir of the tattoo gun going on in the background, so I knew he wasn't too busy.

He wouldn't have answered if there was a client in his chair

His wife would have.

"Ridley's getting his ass kicked at the mall, and Annie's at Hail House without me," I divulged.

"Motherfucker. I'll get everyone rounded up."

I hung up, shoving the phone into my pocket as I straddled my bike.

The bike started up with a thunderous roar, and I was accelerating out of the parking lot within moments of the call.

It was five minutes into my drive when Wolf's bike pulled in behind mine.

I had no clue where he'd come from, but I was happy for his assistance.

I hadn't seen much of Wolf in the past couple of weeks.

His son was having facial surgery that was supposed to correct something to do with his jaw.

When Wolf's son, Nathan, had been a young child, he'd been shot in the head by a serial killer who'd been preying on cop's pregnant wives and family.

Nathan's real father had died, as had Wolf's child and wife.

Wolf had taken Nathan in since his father and Wolf had been best friends, and they'd been together ever since.

Nathan took up a lot more time of Wolf's lately, though, due to his surgery…and I felt like a real shit for not putting in more of an effort with him.

I'd been too busy dealing with my own shit to notice that Wolf looked tired.

I raised an arm at him as a hello, and rode side by side with him until we reached the mall's entrance, pulling in just in time to see Ridley take a punch to the face by a bruiser that had about a hundred pounds on him.

Although it didn't seem possible that anyone could be bigger than Ridley.

Another man was behind Ridley on the ground, and yet another was about ten feet behind him peeling himself up off the fucked up gravel parking lot.

Wolf pulled to a stop only feet away from the downed man trying to get up, and I stopped a couple feet shy of the man trying to beat Ridley to a pulp.

Anyone could beat one trained man with enough people, and it looked like the man still standing hadn't been paying fair.

I picked up the lead pipe that I was fairly sure was responsible for the gash across Ridley's forearm, and took a swing.

It hit the behemoth in the back, across both kidneys, taking him down to his knees instantly.

I wasn't against using whatever I could to gain the advantage.

He'd be pissing blood for weeks.

Yes, I could've easily taken him down without hurting him, but the son of a bitch needed to realize that he couldn't fuck with a cop and get away with it. Especially a man belonging to The Uncertain Saints.

"Fuck," Ridley gasped, putting both of his hands on his knees.

I laughed. "Getting lazy, old man?"

Ridley flipped me off.

"Fuck you. Thanks for comin'," he growled.

I snorted, pulling the cuffs from my back pocket and putting them onto the goliath before lifting him up to his feet.

"Start walking," I snapped when he continued to stay hunched forward.

I knew from experience that getting hit in the kidney hurt like hell, but that was the least of my worries right then.

Wolf was leading his man, cuffed, to the cruiser as well.

It would be a tight fit, but all three men fit like a couple of sardines in a can.

"Alright," I said, walking back to my bike. "Let's go get Annie."

Ridley got into his car and followed me as I hauled ass out of the parking lot to Hail House.

Hail House was a bar and grill owned by Hail Auto Recovery.

It was something they picked up in exchange for a job they'd done for the bank.

They'd done really good for themselves, and as usual, business was

97

booming.

I pulled into the back of the lot, backed my bike into a spot, and started for the front door.

I knew the moment Atticus saw me.

He was working the front door, lazily leaning against the wood beam of the porch.

When he saw me, though, he put the cigarette he was smoking out on the bottom of his shoe and straightened.

"What are you doing here?" He asked casually.

It was anything but casual, though.

It was calculating.

"My girl's here," I told him.

His eyebrows rose.

"You didn't tell her she wasn't supposed to come here?" He shot back.

My hands gripped into tight fists.

There wasn't bad blood between the 'Hail Raisers', as they referred to themselves, and us.

There was, however, a certain rivalry.

A rivalry that sometimes got taken too far.

This time, however, I wouldn't be leaving without Annie.

And Atticus knew it.

Which was why, reluctantly, he let me in.

"She's in the back with your boy," Atticus said.

I raised a brow at him.

"How'd you know he was one of ours?" I asked.

I truly wanted to know.

There are only two places in all of the area that we would tell our prospects to take their cuts off out of respect.

At the Hail House and at the police stations.

Not because we were ashamed or anything, but because we were respectful.

You didn't bring attitude into someone else's house; which was, essentially, what we were doing.

Although Apple hadn't worn his. I knew it even without Atticus' affirmation.

"Boy has a Saint written all over him," Atticus drawled as I passed.

I nodded at him and went in search of my girl and Drew.

I had high hopes for Apple.

He had a good head on his shoulder, and at the age of thirty-five and some change, I knew he'd seen more than most men his age should have to.

He'd been in the military since he was seventeen and had only gotten out two and a half years ago when an IED took off a good chunk of his right upper arm and a portion of his shoulder muscle.

Although, as I walked towards Apple's broad back, I couldn't find a single thing that indicated that he was handicapped in any way.

I knew he trained his body hard to make up for what he saw as his shortcomings.

He was a good man, but he didn't seem to have a grasp on how to deal with women.

Something I realized moments after walking across the entire damn bar to get to them.

Annie had a cup of something clear in her hand that resembled Vodka.

"What kind of name is Apple?" Annie asked as I walked up to where they were sitting.

Drew's back went up.

"It's the kind of name that my momma gave me, and I never questioned it," Drew semi-snapped. "She taught me that it was at the core of a man that counted. Not a name."

That'd been somewhat of a sore subject with our newest prospect. The boys teased him relentlessly about his name, and coming from men, it wasn't anywhere near the same as it was coming from a woman.

A drunk woman, at that.

I hid a smile as I looked down, studying what Annie was wearing.

She had on low riding black jeans that barely covered her curvaceous ass.

A white and black striped shirt

"They should call you Core when you become a member. That sounds a lot more masculine," Annie continued, unaware of the pot she was stirring.

I came up behind her, and I knew the moment she realized someone was behind her because goosebumps started to pop up all over her arms and exposed back.

"Who's behind me, Core?" Annie asked with deceptive calm.

The newly christened 'Core' turned his head slightly, nodding at me in acknowledgement, then he disappeared without another word.

"You shouldn't tease a man about his name. It's not nice," I told her, caging her in with both of my hands against the table at her side.

She stiffened impossibly more.

"Why are you here getting drunk? Who told you about this place?" I asked, leaning down so my mouth ran along the back of her shoulder.

She shivered.

"I h-heard about it from Lenore," she whispered.

I smiled against her skin.

"What else did she tell you about this place?" I asked carefully.

I opened my mouth against her skin, and whatever words she was about to assault my ears with, drifted off the tip of her tongue as if they'd never been.

"Mig," she breathed.

"I've missed you," I told her.

She wouldn't remember that admission in the morning, so that's why I felt free to say what I did next.

"And you need to be careful. I have enemies. I make new enemies every day. But as much as I love you, I'll never expose you to the ugliness of my world. It doesn't matter how much you beg me. There'll never be any time that I'll ever be right for you. It breaks my heart to say this, but you deserve everything. The moon and the fuckin' stars combined. I wish with everything that I am that I could give that to you, but I can't. I'm a street fighter who started to use his fists from ten years of age, and I only got worse from there. Your beauty doesn't belong in my dark world," I whispered into her ear. "But that doesn't mean I won't protect you with my life...and take you out of situations that I know you aren't safe in."

She sniffled, and my heart ached even more to know that I caused her to cry.

However, she got up on her own volition, grabbed her purse, and started to walk out the door.

CHAPTER 11

Fuck the fucking fuckers before the fucking motherfuckers fuck you.
-Text from Annie to Mig

Mig

Atticus' eyes narrowed on Annie before his gaze snapped back up to me.

He must've read the situation, because he didn't say a word as I walked out the door just as quickly as I'd arrived.

Once outside, Apple caught up with me.

He didn't stay by my side, but he stayed close enough that if I needed anything I wouldn't need to yell.

Wolf was still on his bike, gauging the situation.

Annie's sniffles were making my stomach cramp, but she didn't say a single word.

Not even when I led her to my bike.

"Are you okay to ride behind me, or do I need to drive your car home?" I asked.

She finally turned to me, and the look on her face had the breath leaving my body.

God, she looked broken.

And I'd done that to her.

I'd given her the green light, just to rip it away from her at the first sign of trouble.

But I wouldn't budge from this.

At least, that was what I told myself as I helped her onto the back of the bike, mounted in front of her, and rode away.

She didn't hold on to me on the first half of the way to her home.

The only thing that was touching were the insides of her knees around my hips.

And I found that I didn't like that.

Really.

But did I have a right to care about that when I didn't plan to go there with her?

No.

Was I rational when it came to Annie.

Hell no.

I took a corner a little tighter than I usually would, forcing her to wrap her hands around my waist.

She squeaked and scooted forward where she was exactly where I wanted her, and I was finally able to take a deep breath since Drew had called me nearly an hour before.

When I pulled into Annie's store, I waved at Wolf and Drew as they accelerated past me.

Tonight was my night to watch Annie, anyway.

So I'd drop her off, tuck her in like the guy I should be, and watch from the shadows until my relief came.

"Where's your bag?" I asked her in the silence of the night.

"Upstairs. I brought my key and driver's license, though," she answered, getting off and walking to her door.

I followed her, stopping just behind her when she got to the door and unlocked the lock.

What I noticed she didn't do, however, was unarm her alarm.

"You know the point of that alarm, right?" I asked, leaning against the doorjamb.

She shrugged. "Sure do."

I narrowed my eyes. "What, you want to get your place broken into? You want another two by four to the head?"

She leaned forward into my space, giving me a clear view of the tops of her breasts.

"I fail to see how having an alarm would keep me safe from two by fours," she sneered.

I flicked my eyes up to hers, not knowing what to say to her logical words.

I took a deliberate step back until she could easily close the door.

She didn't.

And I had to force myself not to take another step forward.

"Make sure you arm it from now on," I growled.

She sighed.

"The number is like, a million numbers long. It's hard to remember," she admitted.

I took a step towards her alarm.

"You have the number written down?" I asked.

She nodded, walking to the small kitchen table that was in the middle of the back room, pulling her massive bag off the cluttered mess.

She walked back over, digging into her purse until she unearthed a piece of paper, then handed the bag to me.

I was slightly amazed at how heavy the bag was.

I'm talking nearly twenty-five pounds.

How could any woman find that comfortable to carry?

"What do you have in here?" I asked, watching her punch in the buttons. "Rocks?"

She typed the last number and pointed to it.

"There," she said. "You have thirty seconds to leave before it starts freaking out."

I snorted, then started to mess with the system info, holding my hands out for the slip of paper.

She gave it to me, and I punched the numbers in one more time before changing the code completely.

"There," I said. "Now it's easy."

She raised her eyebrow at me in question.

"It's the numbers of your birthdate, followed by mine," I informed her.

She rolled her eyes.

That'd been a funny experience.

We'd learned that our birthdays were on the same day, but I had nine years on her.

She'd teased me of robbing the cradle, and I'd informed her that she'd like my type of cradle robbing.

"Will you hand me a pen out of that bag so I can write it down on another piece of paper just in case?" She asked.

I reached blindly into the bag, freezing when I felt the unmistakable feel of a firearm.

I pulled the cold metal gun out slowly, raising it up so I could get a good look at it.

"Since when did you start carrying a firearm?" I asked.

She shrugged.

"When I got out of the hospital," she answered, turning her back on me.

I closed the door, very intrigued to know the answer as to why she felt the need to carry one.

"Do you know how to shoot this?" I asked, holding up the .40 caliber pistol for her inspection.

"Ish," she wiggled her hand as she made her way to the coffee pot.

I gritted my teeth.

"You don't know how to shoot it?" I asked with incredulity.

She turned to look at me, noticing the tone that my voice had taken.

"I know how. I just don't know if I could actually shoot anyone," she explained.

I growled low in my throat, handing the gun back to her.

"Show me how to unload it," I instructed her.

She took the gun, and I could immediately tell she didn't use it anywhere near as much as she should if she'd planned on carrying it for protection.

She bit her lip, pulling the plump softness in between her teeth.

I watched, cock straining to attention, as she slowly expelled the magazine from the gun, then jacked the bullet from it.

The bullet that was in the chamber hit the floor, and she bent down slowly to pick it up.

I used her inattention to snatch the gun away from her, followed shortly by the clip, loading it and having it ready to fire in less than six seconds.

"Now what?" I asked.

She glared.

"I didn't know I needed to prepare to have you take it from me," she snapped.

I laughed.

"No guy who wants your gun is going to tell you he's about to take it," I informed her dryly.

She pursed her lips, crossing her arms over her ample chest and glared.

With one last look, I handed her the gun and left without another word.

This would be one long night.

***

I was going to die.

Like really, seriously going to die if I had to listen to one more minute of this torture.

I was fucked.

Well and truly fucked.

I'd had the inside of Annie's place wired when she'd moved out of her old house and into the back of her store.

So that meant I not only had a visual but also an ear into what happened in Annie's place.

I don't really know how I'd done it, but when I'd gone to the app to make sure everything was working, like I always did at least once a day, I'd seen something I shouldn't have ever seen.

Annie's naked body.

I'd flinched the moment I saw her, hastily trying to close out of the screen, and in my haste, I'd dropped my phone and shattered the screen.

But the audio on it still worked, which was why I was now staring up at Annie's window, watching the silhouette of her body, and listening to her masturbate to my name.

At first I wasn't sure what she was doing.

I could hear drawers open and close.

The squeaky boards of her floor as she walked across them.

Then the light in the window had turned on.

I'd watched with rapt attention through the curtains, made sheer by the light, as she'd walked to the bed, lifted her leg to place on the edge, and then proceeded to masturbate.

The sounds of her breathing had picked up.

Her cries of pleasure tore through me, making my eyes cross as I gathered my willpower around me and held onto my bike's handle bars for dear life.

Now we were on minute thirteen of masturbation, and my eyes widened as she pulled out a monster of a dildo.

She was helpful by holding it up to the light for me to see, working it over one breast, then the other.

Then she brought it up to her mouth, licked it up and down, then proceeded to lower her hand and run the massive thing up and down the lips of her sex.

Most of it was only my imagination since I couldn't see everything.

I only assumed that was what she was doing, but it wasn't rocket science.

And when she no longer kept the back and forth movement, but switched to the up and down movement, I knew she'd inserted the dildo into her pussy.

Knew it with the same sureness that the sun would rise in the morning.

Her head fell back, and her locks of hair cascaded down her back in rolling waves.

Her free hand lifted, and she plucked at her nipple.

Her breathing hitched, and she started to chant my name like a war cry.

"Mig! Oh, God. Yes, Mig!" She keened.

Even if I hadn't had my phone's audio stuck on, I would've still heard those cries.

And had she screamed anybody else's name in that moment, I would've burst through her backdoor, walked into her room, and then fucked the ever loving hell out of her to inspire her to use only my name from then on.

And then her orgasm was upon her, and she collapsed onto the bed face first.

The only thing I could make out then was her heart shaped ass.

And the only image I could conjure up was my cock lining up with her soft entrance, surging inside, and claiming what should be mine.

The only thing that saved her was the trill of my phone.

I pressed on the screen where my answer button used to reside, and was thankful when the phone immediately stopped ringing, indicating I'd answered the call.

"Yeah?" I grunted.

Griffin's tone didn't sound at all happy.

"Found the ex-husband."

I nodded. "Okay? Where is he?"

"He's dead," Griffin confirmed.

I sighed, rotating my neck to try to alleviate some of my tension that'd just built due to Annie's little show.

"Fuckin' perfect. I'll see you as soon as I can get someone here. Where am I meeting you?"

Yeah, this was going to be a long, *long* night.

Lani Lynn Vale

CHAPTER 12

Somewhere out there there's a tall guy with tattoos, a beard and muscles that likes cuddling as much as I do.
-Text from Tasha to Annie

Annie

"Did you make him think you were stupid in the ways of a gun?" Lenore asked leaning forward.

I had to smile at the way she was standing.

She was leaning against her glass display case where she'd just been stocking her new dildo collection, and with the new position, it looked like she was holding a bouquet of dildos to her chest like the most prized possession.

"Yes," I laughed, pulling my phone out of my pocket and snapping a picture of her. "I did. And he gave me a big old long lecture about gun control and how stupid accidents occur with people who don't know their tits from their hands."

Well, he'd been more tactful than that, but I knew for certain that he wanted to say more than he had.

Griffin, who'd been lazing in a sex swing of all things, snorted.

"I can't believe he was fooled by your act. It won't take him long before he figures it all out. And he won't be happy," Griffin drawled.

I shrugged.

That wouldn't be my fault.

"Then what happened?" She asked.

I blushed, looking covertly at Griffin.

I shouldn't have, because he saw the glance, and grinned huge.

"Well?" He teased.

I blushed harder.

Leaning forward so hopefully only Lenore could hear me, I said, "I masturbated with that dildo I got from you yesterday."

Griffin burst out laughing.

"And let me guess, he heard you?" Griffin guffawed.

I glared at the bastard.

"What are you doing here, anyway?" I snapped.

He held up his hands. "I'm babysitter today."

Ahh, that made sense.

I was still being watched, and he was just making it easier on himself by being in here with his wife and me instead of outside on his bike like the rest of them did.

I'd just opened my mouth to reply to that comment when I saw a police cruiser pull up to the curb and stop in front of my building.

I froze, watching as two cops got out of the car and walked up to my front door and tapped on the glass.

Griffin got up, his face suddenly void of all emotion, and walked to the front door.

When I made to follow, he held up his hand and stayed my forward progress.

"Let me talk to them first, please," he rumbled, pushing through the door and calling out to the officers.

I couldn't tell what was being said, but I was enraptured as Griffin's face flashed from neutral to anger in less than ten seconds as he listened to the cops talk.

Griffin crossed his arms.

"Uh-oh. When he does that, he's putting his foot down about something," Lenore said.

I nervously picked up the first thing I found, nervously squeezing the squishy plastic in my hand while I watched the hub bub outside.

We both moved closer to the glass, watching as the officers spoke animatedly with Griffin.

They'd been going back and forth for maybe five minutes when the loud rumble of a Harley blasted down the street.

"Ten bucks says it's Mig," Lenore teased.

I wouldn't take that bet.

I knew it was Mig.

Just like I knew that this…whatever *this* was…was going to be bad.

Especially if it got Mig hauling ass so loud that I could hear him from the time he got off the main drag in Uncertain.

"Shit," I said, watching as Mig screeched to a halt beside the cop's car.

"Uh-oh," Lenore parroted. "He looks worn and ragged."

He did.

His eyes had dark smudges under them, and I wondered how long he'd been out in front of my shop before he'd left.

Probably all night.

Mig didn't waste time talking to the cops.

Instead, he passed the commotion, letting Griffin deal with it, while he walked straight into Lenore's shop like he owned the place.

"I need to talk to you," he said, not saying a word to Lenore.

Lenore watched Mig walk up to me, then snickered when Mig grabbed my arm and took me to the back room.

The squishy thing in my hand was probably ruined as I squeezed it to death out of sheer nervousness.

"Mig," I started hesitantly.

He slammed the back room's door closed, and then turned to me, studying my face.

"Your ex died last night," he said softly.

My brows rose.

"Really?" I asked.

I wasn't sure why I wasn't freaking out.

I mean, I was married to Ross for two years before our divorce was finalized.

But I couldn't find it in me to be surprised or even upset.

Sure, it was sad, but Ross' death seemed like it'd happened long ago to me, rather than just last night.

"Yeah," Mig confirmed.

"How?" I asked.

I really should be freaking out.

"I sent Casten on the hunt for him after you brought the purses to my attention. He found him the night before last and finally confronted him," Mig said, leaning his back against the counter. "Ross got spooked, scared he would lose the good thing he had going, and he went to the supplier that was giving him the drugs to sell. The supplier felt that he was a loose end that needed tying up, so he shot him twice in the chest at the state park."

I blinked.

"He was dealing drugs with my purses?" I gasped.

I mean, I'd thought he was doing something bad, but it was more like I thought he was just stealing them from people and then selling those to the drug dealers. But no, not Ross.

When he fucked up, he fucked up royally.

No easing into the waters for him.

He was more of a cannon ball type of person.

Then a thought occurred to me.

"How do you know all of this?" I asked carefully.

Mig grimaced, lacing his hands over the top of his head and hunching in slightly on himself.

"To explain this to you, I have to tell you why, exactly, I started putting guards on you in the first place," he said slowly.

My brows rose to my hairline.

"You mean I'm mature enough to know important facts about things that directly involve me?" I said facetiously. "That's interesting."

He gave me a droll look.

"Do you remember the note you were clutching the night you got hurt?" He asked.

My eyes narrowed, and I thought back to the night I'd been knocked out with the piece of wood.

"No," I hesitated. "I don't remember a note at all, why?"

He pulled out his phone, and started pressing buttons on the screen before he turned it around and showed me.

I admired what had to be Mig's new phone before the note on the screen stole my attention.

I read the note, my eyes widening.

"Holy shit!" I gasped. "So how does that note connect to Ross?"

"There was a note with Ross' body. It said three words: Your fault, too," Mig explained tiredly. "The handwriting on this note matches the one that you were holding on to that night. They're identical."

I pursed my lips.

"And do you know who the man is that wrote the note?" I asked, intrigued.

Mig nodded.

"Liam Cornell."

The world dropped out from under my feet.

I placed my hand over my mouth, but the words were out before I could stop them.

"I told you so!"

I was mature like that.

Mig's grin flashed.

"Yeah, you did, didn't you?"

I nodded.

"So how do you know for sure that that was him?" I asked.

"I didn't piss anyone else off lately," he said dryly.

I pursed my lips.

"So what are we going to do now?" I asked.

"We aren't going to do anything. I'm going to take him down with whatever means possible," he countered.

I snorted.

"So this was why you refused to see me anymore?" I asked bluntly.

He frowned.

"I told you last night…you might not remember…" he started.

I held up my hand. "Oh, I remember everything."

He raised his brows at me as if to say, '*well why'd you ask*?' And I laughed.

"That's no reason to stop seeing someone. Seems we'd be better off together rather than separate."

He raised his brow at me, and I suddenly became very aware that we were alone in a room.

And I had a freakin' dildo in my hand, and I was shaking it as I scolded him.

"You can put the weapon down," he held up his hands.

I snorted, tossing it at him.

Which he caught.

Easily.

He examined the dildo in his hand, then looked back at me with amusement.

"It's not mine," I said.

He grinned.

"What kind were you using last night? Do you know that I have your apartment wired? I heard every single moan," he moved closer. "Every single sigh." Closer still. "And every single time you called my name."

By the time he was finished, he had me backed up against the door.

His lower body pinned mine to the door, and I bit my lip as I felt every single inch of him.

Steel hard.

Primed.

Ready.

And that was only his cock.

The rest of him was just as hard, and my hands went up to grip onto his shoulders as I stared into his soulful eyes.

"You're sure you want me? Want this?" He asked, pressing into me.

I swallowed thickly.

I nodded, so very sure that I wasn't hesitant at all.

Not even a little bit.

Then his mouth was on mine.

He ravaged me with only his lips against mine.

It was me who gasped, and my eyes nearly crossed when he swept his tongue inside…stealing away every thought with one single kiss.

He growled into my mouth, leaning down slightly to pick me up.

My legs wrapped around his waist, and I thanked God and every single person that had had a hand in the dress I was wearing. The seamstress, the person that picked the cotton. The fucking plastic model at the store that modeled it so well that I was enticed to buy it.

His rough palmed hand slid up the outside of my thigh, coming to a rest at the curve of my ass.

The other one framed my chin and part of my throat, holding me still for the taking.

His cock, that glorious cock, started to slowly grind into me.

And I gasped into his mouth, stealing the breath from his lungs.

"God," I breathed.

He continued to kiss me, and I could feel my excitement slickening my pussy.

"Oh, my God," I groaned when his mouth left mine, traveling down the length of my throat to come to a stop at my collarbone.

There, he sucked the skin into his mouth, making my eyes cross as I started to really grind down on his cock as much as I could, since the door was at my back.

And then suddenly, this wasn't a kiss any longer.

Any semblance of control flew out the window.

We didn't care that this wasn't the back room of my salon.

We didn't care that the cops were outside wanting to question me about my whereabouts last night.

We didn't care about anything but us.

This.

Now.

Hands started to move, my panties were ripped off of me, then his zipper was lowered.

I bit my lip, watching Mig as he pulled his cock through the opening in his jeans.

Not an easy task.

Especially considering that his cock was not on the small side.

In fact, on a scale from small to enormous, Mig's cock was more on the huge size of large.

It looked angry as it pulsed with each beat of his heart, and I bit my lip, looking into his eyes to see him watching me look at him.

"You're sure? I won't give you back after this," he growled.

"Who would you give me back to?" I breathed, moving my hand down to grip his cock. "And even if there was someone, I wouldn't go back. I've been yours since you moved here."

I used my thighs to lift my hips and placed him at my entrance.

He froze at the mention of me being his since I first saw him.

But I didn't give him time to ask questions; instead, I lined my entrance up with the head of his cock, then sank down onto him.

He helped, of course, lifting me up, then pushing me down.

My pussy stretched, then stretched some more.

My head flew back.

My eyes closed.

And suddenly, with a huge push and jerk, he filled me completely.

I squeaked into his shoulder, biting down with my teeth onto the cord of his neck.

He growled, circling his hips.

Panting, I joined into his rhythm.

What started out as an innocent kiss quickly turned into something very hot and very heavy.

I'd never experienced passion quite like this before.

I wasn't a virgin.

Not even close.

I'd been with five men in my lifetime, but none of them were Mig.

None of them had his skill.

His cock.

His sheer sex appeal.

Add my undeniable attraction to him—and hopefully his for me—and we had something so powerful, *so intense*, I hoped neither of us would be able to go back.

I certainly wouldn't

Not willingly, at least.

If I had my way, Mig and his perfect cock would be mine…forever.

"You're so wet," he whispered into my hair.

I finally let go of his skin, no longer able to hold on when he pulled all the way out, then thrust so hard back inside that my head hit the door.

My back was pushing into the door with such force that a creaking noise was coming from the strained wood with each pump of his hips.

I was panting like I had just ran five miles at top speed while being chased, but at least I wasn't sweating like he was.

This sex between us was real...*raw*.

It wasn't pretty.

It was powerful and life altering.

With each thrust of his cock, he'd hit the back of me, and I swore, it felt like a thousand tiny sparks were skipping down my spine.

I was close, and he could tell.

When he wanted my eyes, he moved his hand that'd been helping support my lower half, and cupped my chin and part of my cheek, holding me captive as he watched my eyes.

I felt like he was delving inside my soul, and I exploded.

"Open your eyes," he growled.

I slowly peeled them open as my pussy started to pulse around his massive length.

I gasped, and he continued to watch as my orgasm rolled through me.

Keeping me right there, in the that moment with him, as wave after waved poured through me.

"Goddammit you have the most perfect pussy," he growled as he came, too.

I was fairly sure he held himself back until I came.

Was that normal for a man like Mig? I don't know, but I wasn't surprised.

He always seemed to have complete and utter control over his body.

He knew exactly what was going on the entire time, and once he knew I'd come, he let himself go, pouring himself inside me.

Pulse after pulse filled me up, and I found myself elated with the knowledge that he'd trusted me enough to let go.

I'd never experienced that feeling before in all my sexual encounters.

Although I'd been on birth control since I was sixteen, I'd never trusted anyone enough to allow them to go without a condom. Even my ex-husband.

And with Mig…I knew it was special.

He knew it was special, too.

"I'm on birth control," I said into the silence of the room.

The only thing that disturbed the quiet was our breathing.

"I know. I saw it last night when you gave me that beach bag of yours," he explained.

I snorted. "It's not a beach bag. It's a purse."

He sighed, pulling back until he could see my face.

His hand around my chin and throat tightened, and then he pulled back all the way.

His cock dislodged from my ravaged pussy, and I groaned at the loss.

"Later," he said, letting me go so I stood on my own two feet.

I nodded.

"You have to go talk to the police," he said. "What they have to say to you is just routine. They'll ask you about where you were last night. I can corroborate that."

I blushed.

He snorted.

"You knew exactly what you were doing. Why be embarrassed about it now?" He teased.

I gathered my dress in my hands and walked awkwardly to the bathroom that was in the very back corner.

After cleaning myself up as best as I could, since sex without a condom is extremely messy, I walked into the backroom, and looked for my panties.

After five minutes of no luck, I walked back into the main room of Uncertain Pleasures, blushing immediately the moment all eyes turned to me.

Lenore and Griffin had knowing smiles on their faces.

The sheriffs, an older man that had to be about fifty or so and a younger guy that couldn't be any more than twenty-one, looked to me in expectantly.

"You're Ms. Autrey?" The older one asked.

I shook my head.

"I don't go by my that name anymore. Now I go by Garcia," I explained helpfully.

The older one nodded.

"I'm Officer Shields and this is Officer Thor," he indicated the younger officer. "We have some questions about your ex-husband."

"Your name's Officer Thor?" I asked, a smile tilting up the corner of my mouth.

Officer Thor nodded.

"I am," he confirmed.

He didn't even smile, and I wondered if he got that a lot.

I wanted to pursue the topic, but I knew when one's closed.

"What can I help you with?" I asked the two.

"Last night around seven p.m. there was a shooting at the mall," Officer

Shields explained. "Your husband was shot twice in the chest."

I blinked. "He didn't make it."

"He did not," Officer Shields confirmed. "Where were you last night?"

I crossed my arms over my chest.

"I was at Hail House until around eight in the evening. Then Mig picked me up and took me home," I answered.

Officer Thor turned to Mig. "You can corroborate that?"

Mig nodded. "I can. I was with her from eight until a little after midnight."

Both officers nodded.

"Do you know anybody that had a problem with your husband?" Officer Thor asked.

I narrowed my eyes at him.

"My *ex*-husband had a lot of problems. He was awful at managing his money. He liked to pick up odd jobs, both illegal and legal. The easier they were to do, the better, since he wasn't particularly fond of working," I told them. "He was pretty good at getting himself into trouble, though."

"That's why you left him?" Officer Thor asked.

I blew out a steadying breath.

"No," I said. "I left him because he liked to screw other women, especially in my bed."

That shut Thor up.

"Is there anything else I can help you with, officers?" I asked. "I have a client coming in soon."

I looked at my watch to see that if I hurried, I'd be able to get all set up before my client got there without being late.

This was a new client coming in, and I wanted to be ready for her when she got here so she'd come back again.

"Thank you for your time," Officer Shields said congenially. "We might have other questions later, if that's okay."

I nodded. "That's perfectly fine."

They both nodded to the men and left, leaving me alone with three people staring at me expectantly.

"What?" I asked.

Mig smiled.

"Do you handle everyone that gets on your nerves like that?" He teased.

I smiled.

"You'll have to wait and see."

CHAPTER 13

Dildos are great, vibrators are fun.
But if you really want a good time,
nothing beats Mig's tongue.
-Annie to Tasha

Annie

I didn't see Mig that night.

Or the next night.

I did, however, have my babysitters.

This time it was Casten.

I didn't know him as well.

"You look tense," I said, looking over at him after he'd shimmied in his seat for the fourth time in less than ten minutes.

"Caught a right hook to the kidney, and my back's been bothering me ever since," he grumbled, rubbing his back with his hand.

I walked over to my table that I'd just cleaned after a visit and patted it.

"Come here and let me work out the knot," I ordered.

He looked skeptical.

"What?" I asked when he didn't move.

"I like my kidneys functioning. And if Mig comes in here and sees your hands on me, he'll make sure they're not," he explained humorlessly.

I snorted and pulled out my phone, pulling up the number I'd snatched from Griffin's phone.

Mig hadn't given me his number, and I hadn't thought to use it until now.

I didn't want to come off as one of those nagging women.

So I'd tamped down my urges and left the phone out of my reach.

Now, though, seemed like an okay time to use it.

I quickly punched out a text and set it on the table.

Casten read the text, and snorted.

Me: Casten won't let me touch him without your permission.

The phone chimed within thirty seconds.

Mig: That's because he's a smart man. What's wrong with him?

Me: His back hurts. Will you let me massage him?

Mig: As long as you promise to return the favor...only give me the sexier version later when I come to your house.

I smiled and showed him the text, and he got up, shucking his shirt off as he moved to the table.

I barely suppressed the breath of air that my lungs wanted to suck in.

Casten was scarred.

Badly.

My sister would go crazy over him.

She had a thing for wounded souls, and there was no way that with the scars marking his body, that Casten wasn't a wounded soul.

"What happened?" I asked carefully, picking up a bottle of lotion.

Casten shot me a wary glance.

"Roadside bomb," he answered shortly, laying onto his belly.

I walked up to the table and was just about to place my hands on Casten's back, but he jackknifed up off the table.

"I changed my mind. I think he wasn't being serious about allowing me to get a massage. I don't want to die," he said quickly.

"Fine," I laughed, moving away from him. "I'll just go play on Facebook while you sit there and hurt."

Casten snorted and sat up, his face set in a grimace as he did.

I washed my hands free of lotion in the sink, then picked up my phone.

My eyes skimmed over the newsfeed, stopping on a picture of a Spanish hunk.

I don't care who you are, if you see a sexy picture of a Spanish God on a newsfeed with the caption, 'Don't watch this at work' as the heading, you're gonna click on it.

I giggled when the man started to speak in Spanish.

I, of course, understood almost instantly what the video was about without even reading the article that was attached to it.

I wouldn't say I was fluent in Spanish, even though both of my parents were.

But I knew the word for 'condom.' 'sex-ed,' 'magnum,' and 'erection.'

I mean, didn't most people?

So without knowing what the entire video was saying, I watched the sexy beast on the screen put on a condom, even though I wasn't alone in the room.

"Jesus," I breathed.

The man on the screen had a big dick.

I'm talking huge.

Although, Mig did, too.

Actually, Mig's cock was probably the same size, if not a small bit larger.

So I watched, captivated, as the man squeezed the condom on over his erection, all the while it never occurred to me once that Casten would be fluent in Spanish and know exactly what was happening on the screen without seeing what was happening.

I watched it two times.

Mostly because I was fascinated with the fact that the guy would do that for a sex-ed class.

Could that be legal?

And would they show that in classrooms?

A noise from across the room had me looking up, not into one pair of amused eyes, but two.

My mouth formed an 'O.'

"What?" I asked nonchalantly.

"Do you need me to show you how to put on a condom so you don't have to watch a video?" Casten deadpanned.

Mig growled.

"No, she most certainly does not," Mig hissed.

Casten snorted. "Then why does she need to watch a video on how to do it? *Twice*. Shouldn't her *man*," that part was said with a snide look in Mig's direction. "Be showing her how to do it?"

Mig flipped Casten off.

And I blushed all the way to my roots.

It never occurred to me that I shouldn't watch the video.

It was right there, waiting to be watched!

I mean, it wasn't like I had gone to a porn site and watched a man jack off.

But as I listened to the two of them argue over Mig's failure to educate me, I rolled my eyes.

Then I did what any red-blooded woman would do.

I watched it for a third time.

By the end of it, though, I had both men watching over my back.

"Good form," Casten said.

Mig snorted.

"What is this?" He asked.

I shrugged, laughing when the guy pulled out a bottle of oil and rubbed it on his condom sheathed cock.

The condom disintegrated.

"Do people actually do that?" Casten asked.

"Apparently, or they wouldn't be warning people not to do it," Mig said dryly.

Once the video was over, I backed out of the video, and continued scrolling through my feed, suddenly very self-conscious.

I hadn't seen Mig since we'd had sex and then he'd had to leave.

He hadn't even called me.

So what was I?

A fuck buddy? A one-and-done?

A girlfriend?

Inquiring minds wanted to know!

"Alright, since you're here, I'm going to go," Casten said. "You gonna be there for dinner tonight?"

"We'll be there," Mig agreed quickly.

"We will?" I asked in alarm. "Where are we going?"

I had plans!

Not ones that I couldn't break, but I didn't really want to!

"Party at the clubhouse," Mig answered, looking at me questioningly.

Was I supposed to know about it?

"And?" I asked.

"And you're going," he ordered.

I snorted. "If you'd have asked me, I might've considered canceling the plans I have with my sister. But not if you're just going to order me."

Casten laughed all the way out of my shop.

Mig, however, wasn't laughing.

His beautiful gray eyes looked even worse when they were mad, and I had the irrational urge to call him Thunder Cloud.

So I did.

"What's your problem, my little Thunder Cloud?" I asked cheerily.

He took a step toward me, and I pushed back in my rolling chair, scooting about three feet back.

He snorted.

"Don't call me your little Thunder Cloud," he said, starting to stalk me now. "And you're going with me."

"But I promised my sister we'd do something together tonight. And I've canceled on her three times now. I can't cancel," I explained, circling around my massage table as fast as I could without tipping myself over onto the ground in a tangle of chair and limbs.

He sighed, as he stopped stalking me; I wasn't going to let him get close to me until I'd had my say.

"Fine," he said. "Bring her with you."

I raised my brow at him.

"You want me to bring my innocent baby sister to a biker party?" I asked.

He grinned, taking a seat on the table.

One foot off the table, while the other was planted on the floor.

"I guess the real question is, do you want me, a newly single man, to be there by myself when you could be there with me?" He challenged.

I stood up and did my own bit of stalking, not stopping until I was inches away from his face.

"My sister's twenty-five going on eighteen. She doesn't know when to stop. She gets a wild hair up her ass to dye her hair, then she goes and dyes it fuckin' tie dye," I growled. "Do you really want to know what'll happen with her at a biker party? She'll fuck Casten, then wind up pregnant, and I'll be babysitting every night because my sister's still in nursing school."

Mig laughed in my face.

"Honey," he laughed. "Your sister's a grown adult. You don't need to keep poking your nose in her business. If she wants to get pregnant by Casten, then let her."

"There will be no getting pregnant with me. Your sister would have to be drop dead gorgeous and I wouldn't touch her with a ten-foot pole. I've sworn off women for the next six months," Casten growled, stalking into the room.

He stopped at the table, picked up his phone, and then stalked right back out.

I grinned at Mig.

"I'll be there. So will Tasha," I said. "You better be ready for Tornado Tasha, because she devours everything in her path." I hesitated. "And Casten is exactly what she doesn't need, but everything she wants."

"You call your sister Tornado Tasha?" Mig asked.

I smiled at him before backing away. "Yes, I do, my little Thunder Cloud."

He glared. I laughed. He grabbed.

And things digressed from there.

Mostly in the form of Mig leaning me over the side of the table, and then letting his mouth travel down my belly.

I moaned when his lips found the exposed skin of my belly, where my shirt had ridden up.

"I like you in leggings," he growled, nipping at my belly.

I giggled, pulling my legs up to wrap around his waist.

He came closer willingly, but he shoved my shirt up in the process exposing my breasts to his hungry gaze.

"Knew you weren't wearing a bra," he growled. "It's a good thing Casten refused to get a massage. I don't like thinking about you pressing your breasts on my brother."

I laughed breathlessly, but it was quickly choked off when his mouth closed over one nipple.

Then his hands started to move.

One went down South, while the other went to my breast, pinching and rolling my nipple in between his fingers.

My back bowed when his fingers slipped underneath the elastic waist of my leggings, moving right past my panties straight into the depths of my pussy.

Mig switched to the other nipple as he slowly worked one thick finger inside me, pulling it out to rub the wetness he'd drawn from my channel over the small bundle of nerves.

My eyes crossed, and I grabbed onto the first thing I could reach, which happened to be Mig's ears.

He didn't seem to mind, though.

Instead, he growled louder as I started to pant.

I'd never particularly liked being fingered.

I hadn't understood that it was more than just fumbling hands which was all that Ross seemed capable of.

Mig, though, did everything with complete and utter focus.

He watched me, felt how my body responded to his touches.

And he knew just when to go slow, or when to speed up.

When to add more fingers inside me.

He paid attention. He knew what I wanted just by reading my reactions.

And both of us were so focused on each other and on what we were doing that neither of us noticed when the office door opened and my sister walked in.

"My God," Tasha exclaimed loudly. "Can I film this?"

I hastily ripped my shirt down over my chest, concealing my breasts.

Mig growled, shielding me with his body as I repositioned my clothes.

Only when I was completely covered, did he sit up.

And neither my sister nor I missed the huge erection that filled out the front of his jeans.

"You must be Tornado Tasha," Mig said.

Well, more like growled, but I wasn't going to get into semantics.

"Seriously, Annie? Why do you have to tell everyone that?" She asked, walking into the room like she didn't just catch me on the verge of having sex with a hot and sexy man.

I smiled at her, nearly spontaneously orgasming when Mig brought his fingers to his lips while my sister had her back turned and licked my juices off his fingers.

My mouth dropped open.

He grinned.

Then he was gone, leaving me with a smirking Tasha.

"So…you have something to tell me?"

CHAPTER 14

I don't have a bucket list. However, my fuck-it list is novel length.
-Mig to Annie

Mig

"Do you think when a mattress is on top of a car, it's a prostitute making house calls?" Annie asked her sister.

My head turned, and a laugh bubbled up my throat.

Amazingly, I was able to hold it in.

Annie was notorious for making random comments like that, and when alcohol loosened her tongue, she said even more ridiculous comments than she normally would.

"No," Tasha said. "That's just weird."

"But why else would someone put it on top of their car?"

Peek was laughing uproariously at the way our conversation had turned.

I'd made a comment, not even a minute before, how Annie couldn't keep her mind on the task she was given if you got her distracted, and he didn't believe me.

So to prove my point, I started talking about how I wanted to go mattress shopping, and she'd gone off on a tangent about prostitutes and mattresses.

"Annie," I said sharply.

She looked up at me with wide, brown eyes.

"Yeah?" She asked.

"Do you have the chicken ready yet?" I asked, knowing without a doubt that she didn't.

She looked down at the chicken that was still just as fatty now as it had been when I handed it to her ten minutes before.

"No," she said. "I'm working on it."

"Mine's done!" Tasha exclaimed.

I turned my eyes to Tasha, struck once again how different she was from Annie.

Where Annie was short, Tasha was tall.

I'm talking five or so inches over Annie's five feet four inches.

Annie had lovely curves, and a beautiful abundance of breasts to work with, whereas Tasha could maybe fill up a B...if she was lucky.

They did have the same wavy, curly-when-it-wanted-to-be, brown hair.

But their eyes were different colors.

Annie's were a warm shade of honey brown, while Tasha's were a darker shade that looked almost black.

And their attitudes.

Swear to Christ.

Tasha was a little timid, looking at the gathering with wide, nervous eyes.

She looked like she'd never been out amongst the general population before...and maybe she hadn't.

Annie, though, my sweet Annie, was easy going, got along well with Lenore and the rest of the club. Didn't sneer at the women that showed for the party...nor the men.

Not that I cared if she got along with the men.

She stayed by my side, keeping her eyes, as well as her attention, on me.

Tasha had loosened up after Annie had poured some drinks down her throat.

Not that Tasha had realized there was any booze in her drinks.

She'd been told they were lemonade.

And Annie had laughed behind my back as Tasha had drank one after the other.

Now, though, Annie was just as sloshed as Tasha, and the boys were enjoying the shit out of it.

"That chicken is butchered," Annie laughed. "There's more chicken on the fat you cut off than on the chicken that we're supposed to cook."

I looked over at Tasha's chicken, and thought that just maybe it hadn't been a good idea to give a knife to two drunk girls.

"It's alright," I said, taking Tasha's knife. "I'll cut these up. How about you ladies go take a seat next to Lenore."

Lenore was sitting on the couch with Griffin sitting beside her, rubbing her pregnant belly like one would a pet.

She looked cute…and it made me think of Jennifer.

Of my child.

This life I'd been given was not how I'd expected it to play out.

If I had ever thought about a woman carrying my child, I'd have seen myself doing much the same as Griffin was currently doing.

Never in my life would I have imagined myself watching my child grow in the belly of a woman that I despised.

"So I have some news for you, and I'm not sure you're going to like it,"

Casten said once the women left to take up seats across from Griffin and Lenore.

I looked over at him, then back down at the chicken.

"You looked deeper into Cornell? Autrey?" I asked.

He'd told me he was going to do it.

We'd gone the official route, and, of course, there was little to nothing new there to be found. So Casten started to dig deeper, unofficially, of course.

Casten was a bounty hunter.

He'd found Ross Autrey for me, not that it had done much good, though. Then he'd started looking into Liam Cornell.

I hadn't expected any news at this point, and it somewhat surprised me that he already had some.

It'd taken him days to find anything on Autrey.

Whomever was covering their tracks was good.

"Yeah," he said, leaning his hips against the kitchen counter next to me. "I had to double check…but what I found…it's bad."

I sighed and put down the knife, walking over to the sink to wash my hands.

Once they were clean of chicken guts, I started out the door.

Casten followed me silently.

Once outside, I saw Apple talking to someone on the phone.

"Yo," I snapped. "Core!"

Apple turned around like his ass had been cattle prodded.

"Yes?" He asked, hanging up on whomever he was talking to.

I grinned.

"Go cut up those pieces of chicken. Try not to make them any smaller than they already are," I ordered.

Core, who'd we'd just started calling that since the night he'd helped me with Annie at Hail House, practically ran inside.

"I kind of like that name. Wish I would've gotten something cool like that," Casten said.

I snorted.

Casten had been dubbed 'Big Ten'. something he never went by because he said it made him sound like a surfer.

Ours wasn't really the type of club that cared what you wanted to go by.

You went by what you wanted to go by, and that was that.

"Tell me what you got," I said softly.

He opened the file that he magically pulled from his back pocket, and my stomach rolled.

***

Casten roared off the second Tasha was clear of his bike, not even looking backwards to make sure she was safely on the concrete.

I laughed under my breath, getting off my bike as I did.

The man had it bad, and he didn't stand a chance.

Seriously, there was nothing a man could do if one of the Garcia sisters put you in her sights.

All Casten could do was hold on for the ride.

Annie waved goodbye, and I walked slightly behind Tasha to her front door.

"Don't forget that you promised to help me out tomorrow with practice,"

Tasha said as an afterthought.

I looked back in the direction I'd left Annie, who smiled and waved at her sister in acknowledgement.

"I'll be there…with bells on!" She screamed.

Tasha snorted and continued to walk, glancing at me once we got to the door.

"You're not going to hurt her, are you?" Tasha blurted suddenly.

I blinked.

"Not intentionally, no," I replied softly.

She nodded, studying her feet for quite a while before she looked up at me, smiled, then went inside without a backwards glance.

I turned and walked away once I heard the doors lock, heading to my bike where Annie was leaning over, playing with the key chain.

"What are you doing?" I said loudly, making her jump with a guilty look on her face.

"I'm sorry," she laughed. "I just like your keychain.

I nodded.

"It was a bullet I got in Iraq," I said, not offering up an explanation as to why it was on my keychain.

I knew she wouldn't let it go.

Although, I'd hoped she'd leave it alone, I knew she wouldn't.

Annie just wasn't made that way.

She was always thirsty for information. Curious.

Especially when it came to me.

"You were in Iraq?" She asked.

I laughed.

"Yeah, you could say that," I responded evasively.

I wouldn't be telling Annie about my time there.

Not tonight. Not after we'd had such a good time together.

One day she would have to know more about Iraq and my deployments, but not right now. We were too new. We had too many things we needed to work on first before we started on the demons of my past.

Annie must have realized that Iraq was a sore subject, because she smiled and turned around towards the bike.

"Don't forget to get her up by eight. The game starts at nine," Tasha ordered, making us both turn to look back at the opened door.

Annie waved at Tasha, acknowledging that she'd heard.

"Where does she have to be?" I asked.

"The high school. Tomorrow is the alumni volleyball game at our old high school," Annie replied, smiling slightly.

My thoughts immediately went to tight little shorts, and how fuckin' hot they would look cupping Annie's ass.

It didn't surprise me that Tasha had been a volleyball player.

Tasha may be a knockout, but she had nothing on Annie.

Annie who was short and curvy.

I hadn't realized that short girls played volleyball.

"We'll get you there on time."

Annie smiled and remounted the bike. She sat there with her eyes closed.

"Helmet!" I barked.

"Shit," she said, covering her heart. "You scared me."

I smiled down at my feet as I straddled the seat in front of her, waiting patiently for her to slip the helmet onto her head.

"Sorry," I said once she was situated.

She wrapped her hands around my waist.

"I wasn't truly asleep, but really close to being there," she admitted.

I patted her thigh.

"Your place or mine?" I asked.

She squeezed me tighter.

"Where is yours now?" She asked curiously.

In answer, I started the bike and headed back towards the river.

I was staying on a house boat.

One that Griffin had been staying at during his and Lenore's separation.

Not that the separation had gone on for long.

Seemed the houseboat was bound and determined to kick its occupants out before they thought they were ready to commit to relationships.

The haze of clouds made the ride feel ominous, but Annie seemed to enjoy it, despite it being on the cooler side.

We arrived at the clubhouse once more, and she was practically asleep on my back.

And by the time I'd motored across the lake on the boat, she *was* asleep.

How, I didn't know.

The river was louder than fuck, and it wasn't a gentle ride.

The wind was picking up, and waves were white capping, but Annie didn't budge, and I wondered idly if she'd make it to her game in time in the morning.

A quick ride from the clubhouse to the house boat, I tied us up while Annie, out like a light, snored softly, not a care in the world.

Her complete trust in me was humbling.

But for the first time in a very long time, since my first deployment in Iraq, I was afraid.

I was afraid not only for Annie, but also for me.

After reading what Casten was able to uncover about not just Liam Cornwell, but my ex-wife as well, I was left reeling.

And I wasn't sure how the hell I was going to get myself out of this without leaving a huge, gaping hole in my heart.

CHAPTER 15

*When I'm through with you, even the neighbors will need a
cigarette.*
-Mig's secret thoughts

Mig

"What the fuck are we doing here?" Casten asked, walking beside me
down the corridor of Jefferson High School.

"Exactly what I want to know," Wolf grumbled.

I took Nathan from Wolf's hands, delighted to hear him giggle for the
first time in weeks.

"Because, for some reason, I was roped into it," I said, blowing a
raspberry into Nathan's neck.

He was looking really good, and I was happy to see that he'd started to
come back to his old self.

"How was a six foot three motherfucker, such as yourself, 'roped in' to
anything?" Ridley asked.

I waited until we made it into the gym, entering the door that Annie told
me to enter through, and pointed.

"That," I answered, pointing at Annie's small shorts that covered slightly
more than panties would.

"Damn," Casten hissed, his eyes going to Tasha.

Tasha was wearing much the same as Annie was.

Short shorts that could double as a pair of those boy shorts underwear, a ribbed tank top, knee pads, long socks that came up to her knees, and white shoes the likes I'd never seen before.

I snorted, then walked to the bleachers, stepping up on the first bench to take a seat on the second.

The shoes reminded me of those old 80's shoes that the women used to wear to work out in, offering what I guessed was ankle support.

I had to admit, Tasha looked good.

But she wasn't Annie.

"The little high school girls aren't doing it for me, but motherfucker, look at the other side," Ridley drawled, looking at a young woman who was still in incredible shape, even though it was blatantly obvious that she hadn't been in high school for a while.

"My eyes haven't made it past that ass," Casten mumbled, mostly to himself.

"So why did the cops get called out to your house this morning?" Ridley asked, keeping his eyes on the woman.

I sighed, shifting Nathan onto the floor between my legs.

He immediately got down and started across the court.

Annie, having seen the little boy, broke off from where she'd been setting a ball, and picked Nathan up.

Nathan and Annie had met at the party last night, and Annie had fallen in love.

Nathan had a way of making women melt, so it wasn't much of a surprise.

"Nate!" Annie crowed, bending down to gather the boy into her arms.

Nathan squealed, and Annie took him to a cart that was holding about fifty balls, pulled one out and handed it to him.

He wrapped his chunky arms around the ball as far as he could, then laid his head against the top of it.

I turned away from the sight of her holding a baby.

My God, how I wished, yet again, it'd been her that I'd gotten pregnant.

Things would be so much simpler, easier—*happier*—if it were her carrying my child.

"We went to my place last night, so this morning I had to make a hasty trip by her old place, next to my house, to get her some clothes she was storing there, to wear to this," I said. "And when I pulled up on my bike, Jennifer, who was home at the time, came out of my front door thinking I was there to see her…which I wasn't. I'd originally intended to meet with her this morning to confront her about what Casten showed me last night, but I called and canceled when Annie asked me if I wanted to come with her."

"And she got pissed," Casten said dryly.

I nodded. "She got pissed."

Wolf chuckled when his son threw the ball, causing Annie to bend over for it.

He continued to do it, too, thinking it was a fun game.

I, of course, thought it was awesome.

Annie kept bending over, giving me a fine show.

"Needless to say, she started wailing and carrying on, accusing me of cheating with our neighbor. Called me every name in the book," I continued. "And the old woman on the other side of my house called the cops."

Ridley nodded.

"Not really sure what she expected. You can't just scream profanities in your yard like that. I could have charged her with disturbing the peace," Ridley growled.

I clapped my hand down on his shoulder causing him to jerk forward slightly.

He glared at me.

"What?" He asked. "She would've deserved it."

She would have, but I was trying not to be petty.

"Thought she was going to have a coronary when I told her to stop it," Ridley continued.

"Why didn't she?" Wolf asked.

I snorted. "She probably would have, but I got her calmed down enough that I could get gone before she could start back up again."

"The last time you gave into her temper, you ended up marrying her," Casten observed.

I sighed.

"He told her he'd go to her doctor's appointment this afternoon," Ridley said when I didn't answer fast enough.

Casten laughed.

"You're so fucked. You won't be able to keep Annie for long. She's not going to put up with your shit...nor your ex's," Casten informed me.

"I'm taking her with me, and you're right. She wasn't happy. But Jennifer doesn't get a say so in how I live my life anymore, not when she's in bed with the fuckin' devil," I ground out.

"You think she knew what she was doing at the time?" Wolf asked.

A whistle pierced the gymnasium's air, and I looked up to find Annie hurrying toward me.

She had Nathan on one hip, and she was smiling as she walked quickly towards Wolf.

"I'll let him keep the ball, but try not to let him throw it on the court. He might kill one of us since we're so rusty," Annie snickered, handing Nathan over.

Wolf took Nathan and sat him on the bleacher between his feet. "Don't throw the ball, boy, or you'll get me in trouble with the pretty lady."

Annie laughed softly, raised a hand up to her face, then blew a kiss in my direction

I smiled, barely resisting the urge to 'grab' it out of midair and paste it to my lips.

I was not that far gone...*yet.*

"So how does this volleyball game work?" Wolf asked as the girls lined up.

I shrugged. "I thought you just hit it over the net. There are rules?"

"You get three hits," Casten said, surprising both of us. "One player serves it to the other team, and they have three touches to get it back over the net and grounded on the serving team's side for a point. And you can't go out of that little box around the court once it goes to the other side. There is a little more to it than just that but, you get the idea."

"How do you know all that?" Wolf asked what we were all thinking.

"My sister. I used to have to go to her practices since she was my ride home," Casten explained.

He sounded like he didn't want to talk about it.

Not even a little bit.

So we let it be and watched the game being played in front of us.

The high school team was good, I'd give them that.

But they weren't the alumni.

Even without practicing, according to Annie, they still had incredible skill.

And although they were rusty at first, they played like a well-oiled machine.

Sadly, the varsity girl's team didn't know what hit them.

"Perfect dig," Casten muttered, his eyes fascinated.

The 'perfect dig' was received by Annie, who placed it perfectly in the girl at the front's hands.

The next play happened so fast that I wasn't even sure what was happening.

"Block! Block! Middle!" The assistant coach screamed loudly.

The girls scrambled, having misread the direction that the setter was placing the ball.

And Tasha flawlessly arced around the setter, then proceeded to slam the ball down the girl's throat.

It hit the ground with such force that the ball bounced at least fifteen feet in the air.

"Holy shit," Casten said.

I concurred.

That was awesome.

"Wonder why she quit. She could be a professional," Wolf observed.

"*She's* the coach. The woman that's up there now is the assistant coach," I said.

Casten's eyes came to me.

"She's the girls' volleyball coach? I thought she was in nursing school," Casten said.

I nodded.

"She is. But she's also working full time," I agreed. "Annie says she's a perpetual student, and has three degrees now."

She was only a year younger than Annie's twenty-six, and I also wondered how she'd gotten so many degrees at such a young age, but I never asked

Casten, however, was intrigued.

I could see it the way his shoulders had shifted, following Tasha's movements the way I did Annie's.

Annie switched positions when the girls finally scored on the alumni, and she was switched out with one of the other players.

This one was taller than Annie, and she took her position on the front row closer to the net.

Annie sat down next to a smiling girl who looked on the verge of being too thin, animatedly talking to her while she gestured to the court.

The game continued around us, and as soon as Tasha was switched out, our topic of conversation turned to a case Griffin, Wolf and I were working on.

"Could you please stop speaking so vulgarly?" A snotty woman's voice said from beside me.

I turned to find a woman that looked like the proverbial soccer mom, or in this case volleyball mom.

"What?" I asked.

She sneered. "You've said the F word no less than four times in the last three sentences. Please stop speaking like that or leave. And why on earth are you wearing those gang jackets to a school function?"

My brows rose.

"I'm sorry, I wasn't aware that there was assigned seating. If I remember correctly, I was here first. You were the one who sat down next to us," I said plainly.

She narrowed her eyes.

"I'll have you know that my brother is the sponsor for this team, and damn near every sporting event in the school. And I'm sure he'd be more than willing to talk to your boss," she hissed.

I laughed.

"Lady, do you know who I am?" I asked.

She sneered.

"You're the guy who left his pregnant wife for another woman," she hissed.

I turned my face forward, anger boiling to the surface like lava about to erupt from a volcano.

Out of everyone in the room, I would've expected the blowup from any one of the boys at my side.

What I didn't expect, though, was it to come from Annie.

A ball flew within arms reach of my face.

I could've reached out and slapped it away, had I been expecting it. But I hadn't, which was why the chick at my side got a face full of volleyball.

"Shut your mouth, woman! You don't know what you're even talking about! So before you open your mouth in the future, make sure you know what you're actually talking about and have your facts straight before you spread gossip and lies about people!" Annie growled.

I blinked, turning to see Annie standing about five feet from me, another ball in her hand ready to launch.

Which she didn't waste time doing.

She reared back and threw it again, but this time I was quick enough to catch it before it could hit the woman at my side for a second time.

"Now, Annie," I chided laughingly.

She glared at me.

"How can you defend that…that horrid, awful woman while she sits there spewing those lies? I had not one thing to do with your marriage ending, and I certainly didn't break up your home. And, she doesn't know a goddamned thing about your life or mine, and she shouldn't be spreading lies and gossip like that!" Annie spat.

The woman got up, turning to face us both. Her face obviously angry and eyes narrowed as she spoke. "Oh, you're going to regret this, I'll make sure of it. My brother will see to it that no one, not one single person, sets foot in your salon ever again. You can kiss your business and your home-wrecking life goodbye!" The lady sneered at Annie.

I wondered idly how long Ridley was going to let this go on, but when the young girl I presumed was the woman's daughter started to cry, it was Casten, of all people, that got up.

"This isn't the time nor the place for this. It's time to go," he ordered, starting forward.

"Don't you dare touch me!" The woman hissed and she yanked her arm away from Casten before he could touch her. She turned on her heel, and stormed out of the room, leaving the distraught girl trailing slowly behind.

"Well," Annie huffed, "that was a lot of fun."

I moved forward, to grab hold of her hand before she could move away, and laid a wet, possessive kiss on her mouth.

"Finish up," I ordered. "I've got a few things I want to do."

Her brows rose. "Oh yeah? What's that?"

I didn't answer her, I just walked back to the bleachers and took a seat once again.

She stared at me the entire way, only turning back to the game when Tasha called her name.

For the remainder of the game, we just admired the view and kept our talk to things that didn't have anything to do with what had just happened.

Once they were done playing, we went outside to wait for Annie and Tasha.

They must have hurried because it wasn't long before Annie was back in my arms.

"You did good, baby," I growled against her neck.

She tasted of salt, the sweat on her skin having dried in the time she'd spent talking to all the younger players.

"So what now?" She asked. "I've got an hour before I have to be in the salon."

I shook my head. "I'm have to drop you off early…I'm sorry, I have to deal with Jennifer."

She visibly slumped.

"I was afraid you were going to say that."

***

Jennifer looked positively contrite when I arrived at her house an hour later.

"I'm sorry," she whispered. "I know I was out of line."

I wanted to laugh in her face.

Of course she was out of line. That was what she did.

She was so out of line, so often that I wouldn't be surprised if my friends called her Out Of Line Jennifer.

"I have some questions for you," I said tersely, looking at all the shit she had laying around.

It was as if she'd given up cleaning all together when I left, and by the looks of all the take out menus, scattered around, she stopped cooking, too.

"I have to go to a doctor appointment, do you…are you still going with me?" She asked softly.

I shrugged. "Yeah. That's fine."

The conversation I wanted to have probably shouldn't be discussed at a doctor's office, but I thought that just maybe it'd keep her from throwing a huge fit.

We drove the hospital in my truck that I hadn't moved from under the carport since I'd left.

As I parked and got out to walk, I wasn't immune to the looks Jennifer and I got.

Jennifer was beautiful and pregnant, she was stunning.

People looked at us like we were the perfect couple.

Oh, if they only knew!

I hurried to take a seat, and Jennifer didn't take the one next to me, instead sitting a few seats over.

We sat in silence for five minutes until a nurse called her back.

"You must be so excited. You only have a few more weeks to go!" The nurse said happily. Then, she turned her eyes to me. "I've been wondering when you'd show! She always telling us how proud she is of you."

I gave Jennifer a look that clearly said everything I was feeling, and she looked away with embarrassment.

We waited for the nurse to get done taking Jennifer's blood pressure, checking the baby's heartbeat and asking if Jennifer had any concerns.

"I've been having what I think are Braxton hicks, but my back's been hurting for going on a week now," she said.

That was news to me.

I may not like her very much, but I didn't want anything to happen to her.

Which reminded me that I needed to get to the point of why I was here with her in the first place.

"Okay, I'll let the doctor know. He may or may not want to check you," she said.

I was hoping for not.

I wanted to talk to her, and if he had to check her, I'd have to leave.

"Thank you," Jennifer said formally.

The nurse smiled and patted her arm, and I wanted to scream at the nurse about how manipulative Jennifer was.

She could make anyone like her.

Anyone.

Well, except me.

I didn't like her.

Then again, neither did my brothers.

The moment I was left alone with Jennifer, I pulled out a note and handed it to Jennifer to read.

Her eyes widened, and her head hung like I'd gutted her where she sat.

"This man approached me, offered me two hundred thousand dollars to sleep with you. To get some information out of you. I got him your number. Your address off your driver's license. Little things like that." Jennifer's lip trembled, and I never wanted anything more but to put her in her place.

I kept my cool. Barely. She was pregnant with my child after all, and I would never actually hurt her…at least not physically.

"Go on," I said shortly.

"At first, he just wanted me to sleep with you so he could get pictures of us to blackmail you with should they ever get busted." Jennifer whispered brokenly. "But when I got pregnant, he decided it would be better to have access to you anytime they wanted it. They planned to use our child to make that happen."

White hot rage boiled underneath the surface of my carefully calm exterior.

"And that was okay with you?" I asked carefully.

Her eyes met mine, and she looked grief stricken.

"I took every possible precaution when it came to you. I put on a condom for you. I had an IUD. I never intended for this to happen. I just wanted to take care of my…problem, to make it go away," she cried. "I just wanted to get off of drugs."

I crossed my arms over my chest.

"And how'd that work out?" I asked.

She shook her head.

"I kicked the drugs in rehab, right before I realized that I was pregnant.

So, in a roundabout way, my original problem is gone, but, well, new ones have since emerged," she admitted.

Ain't that the fuckin' truth.

"Why tell me now?" I asked, staring at her stomach.

Oh, how I wished this would've happened with Annie.

I wanted Annie to be the woman carrying my child, and not this deceptive bitch in front of me.

"I should be having the baby any day now…and I wanted you to know…in case Marco tries something," she whispered.

I looked away from her to the wall beyond her head.

"You're going to sign the paper relinquishing all parental rights to this child and giving sole custody to me. You will leave and never look back. You'll never try to contact us again, ever. And by us, I mean me, the baby, Annie, my friends. Anyone in my life at all. I'll get you out. I have a plan in motion through some contacts who can and will make you disappear. You'll do everything they tell you to do, exactly as they instruct you to do it, and you'll be able to live your life with a clean slate and a fresh start," I said slowly, succinctly, making myself clear and leaving no room for negotiation.

Jennifer started to sob.

"But I-I-I want m-my baby. She s-saved my life," she cried.

I just stared at her.

"I am a law enforcement officer, Jennifer. You actively colluded with a drug dealer to drug me with the intent of raping me in order to get photographs for this dealer to use in an attempt to blackmail me. Despite your precautions, you became pregnant as a result of your role in these crimes against me. Now you have a drug dealer on your back who will not hesitate to use the baby to get to me directly and to keep you in line to get to me indirectly. There is no way that you can safely participate in the baby's life without putting either of you in danger. To avoid either becoming the dealer's puppet for life or the possibility of prosecution for your crimes, your only real option is to run, to never look back and to start over. Don't you agree?" I asked carefully.

She shook her head vehemently. "No, you're r-right. I'll do it, I'll go. And, Mig, I… I'm sorry. If that's even worth anything to you now."

I shrugged. "Maybe some day it'll mean something. But right now, everything you told me is just too fresh and new. You raped me. I just don't understand how doing that to me—to anyone—was a fair price to pay so you could get drug money. Most likely, I'll never understand."

She cried harder.

The doctor came in, and he looked at Jennifer with sympathy.

"Hormones make a lot of women cry uncontrollably," the doctor said, misunderstanding the situation.

I didn't correct him, because, honestly, I had no idea how to tell the doctor that the minute the baby was born, I intended to take her as far away from Jennifer as I could get her.

He'd wonder why, and then I'd have to lie, because no matter what, I would never make Jennifer out to be the devil.

"The nurse tells me that you're having a back ache?" The doctor asked.

Jennifer nodded.

"Yeah, it's been like this for the past week," she replied.

And as I left the doctor's office with a still sobbing Jennifer twenty minutes later, I was seriously regretting the decision not to tell the doctor just how much I disliked Jennifer and why.

Lani Lynn Vale

CHAPTER 16

Every man either needs to stand up and be the man she needs you
to be, or sit the fuck down so the man behind you can see her.
-Fact of Life

Annie

"No. Just no," I said, shaking my head vehemently. "I'm not doing it."

"She doesn't have anyone else. And I don't have another choice. Please don't do this to me," I pleaded.

She glared at me.

"Why do I have to be there? Why can't I stay at my own place? What about my dog?" I countered.

Mig's eyes narrowed.

"Because I don't want to be there either. Unfortunately, someone needs to be around for Jennifer, since she was placed on bedrest and there isn't anyone else, except me. And if you're there, it'll be a little bit more bearable," he said evenly. "And we could move to your place above the salon, but it would be cramped for space. I'll do either one that makes you more comfortable."

"Why don't you hire someone to watch over her?" I challenged.

He sighed and looked out the window.

"I tried that. And would do that, but it's going to cost a fuckin' whack, and I just bought some new land, and then put all the money down on a house that'll be built within the next six months. I don't have the money to spare," he said defensively.

My head, which had been in my hands, went up slowly.

"You bought some land and a house?" I asked in alarm.

He nodded.

"Where?" I wondered.

"Off the highway. It butts up to the lake," he said, pulling out his phone.

We spend the next ten minutes trying to decide where to put a house, and I had to say I was excited.

I'd never seen a house built from nothing.

I thought it'd be a fun experience to witness, even if it wasn't my house.

"Are you going to go more modern or contemporary?" I asked, looking through Pinterest now for house plans.

"I don't know. What do you like?" He asked randomly.

I shrugged.

"I like a more rustic look, but with a modern feel to it," I told him.

He nodded.

"That's kind of what I like, too," he said, leaning over my back to look at the pictures I was looking at.

"Well, since you know what I like, maybe you can help me pick out some of the designs. I have to go, not tomorrow, but the next day to a few different appointments to pick out the flooring, cabinetry, and lights," I said. "I want you to come with me."

I nodded, then finally broached the subject that was really bugging me.

"You know it's a form of torture, right, asking your present fuck buddy to live in the same house as your ex?" I said cautiously.

166

I wanted to move in with Mig, I really did.

In fact, it was at the top of my 'things I want to do the most' list.

We only got to see each other now for little snippets of time.

If I were living with him, I'd see him in those in between times, as well.

And I wanted that.

But what I didn't want was to watch Mig wait hand and foot on Jennifer because she was on bed rest.

Mig grabbed my phone, tossing it onto the dresser, and drawing my attention.

I blinked when I looked up to find my face only inches from Mig's.

"What?" I asked somewhat nervously.

"You're not my fuck buddy," he growled. "In fact, you couldn't be further from my fuck buddy."

Hurt flashed across my face, and he saw it before I could hide it.

"Okay," I whispered.

"That's not what I meant, so get those stupid thoughts out of your head," he ordered roughly. "What I meant was that you're my woman. Not my fuck buddy. So, of course, your opinion matters to me. If you really don't want to live with her, then I'll deal with it. I'll go hire a caretaker even if I have to take out a loan to do it."

I'd offer him the money if I had it, but I was fairly positive he wouldn't take money from me.

In fact, I doubt he'd take it from any of his friends, so I didn't feel slighted.

"I'm your woman?" I asked hesitantly.

He laughed.

In my face.

Like a rude ass.

"You've been my woman since you moved in next door. I may have been married…as well as you, but my heart was yours from the moment you dropped your end of the couch. I know you don't want this. I know it. But I am only trying to find the best solution to this mess." He hesitated, "I was going to ask you to move in with me…or the other way around, since I currently live on a houseboat the size of a postage stamp. This isn't ideal, I know, but it's real. Our real."

I closed my eyes.

"Can y'all move here?" I asked. "I have a spare bedroom, and I think with all my things here I'll feel more comfortable."

He nodded, cupping my face.

"Yeah, we can do that," he agreed.

"And don't expect me to wait on her hand and foot. If she needs something, you're getting it, got it?" I growled.

He smiled and leaned forward.

"Got it."

He leaned forward more.

"And she better not be mean to my dog," I snapped. "That's Katy's room. Katy gets to stay if she wants to stay."

His lips were a hairsbreadth away now, and I was breathing faster in anticipation.

"Would never dream of it."

"And you need to talk to her about her mouth. If she starts talking trash about you or me, or you and me, I'll let her have the edge of my tongue," I hissed.

He'd told me everything that had happened today at the hospital. Starting with her explanation as to why she'd raped Mig, and ending with the discussion the doctor had had with her about needing bed rest. So while this may not be an ideal situation, I know Mig wants this baby healthy, and I'll do what I have to in order to see this through.

"I guess I should be happy it's only for two more weeks rather than two more months," I muttered.

His mouth crashed down on mine, and I found myself, back to the bed, beneath Mig's large, sexy, hard body.

He settled his slim hips in between my now splayed thighs and deepened the kiss.

My heart rate, already racing in my anger, started pounding.

Thud. Thud. Thud. Thud.

I gasped into his mouth, fighting for breath.

Slickness started to coat my sex in preparation for him, and my legs involuntarily rounded his hips to bring him even closer.

His hard cock ground into my mound.

He was so hard that it hurt.

It was a good hurt, but a hurt nonetheless.

I liked it.

In fact, I liked it so much that I barely registered the yelling at first.

Only when Mig stopped did I realize that what I'd been hearing didn't belong to the TV in the background, but to the woman on the other side of the clubhouse.

Mig had brought Jennifer here because it was neutral territory for both her and I, and I'd showed up later and nearly had a meltdown at what I saw.

Mig had been across the room from Jennifer. She was laying on the couch like a queen waiting to be pampered.

When I'd arrived, he'd immediately gotten up and dragged me to the bedroom, where we now stood.

"I need to go to the bathroom!" Jennifer screeched.

Mig's eyes narrowed, both of us panting as we tried to decide what to do next.

Mig's cock was harder now as he looked down into my eyes, but Jennifer's voice was getting louder.

I smiled at him, then made my decision.

I reached down and started to push my pants down.

Mig stiffened his arms beside me and lifted his legs, one at a time, to allow me to move my pants down.

My panties followed my pants, and soon I was bared to his gaze.

He licked his lips, and started to lower himself back down on top of me, but Jennifer interrupted him once again.

"Please! I don't know where the bathroom is!" She yelled.

Mig's eyes narrowed.

I had a feeling that she knew exactly where the bathroom was.

Swear to Christ, the door was right off the main room she was in. There was no way she didn't see it from the couch.

So, once again, I made the decision to try to capture his attention once again.

I wanted to prove a point, not just to him, but also to Jennifer.

She would not have him at her beck and call.

Nowhere in the fine print did the doctor say that she needed to be waited on hand and foot.

So as I eased my hands down Mig's taught abdomen, then slipped my hands under the waistband of his jeans as I peppered his bearded jaw with small kisses.

"Mig," I breathed against his skin.

He looked down at me as I eased the zipper down, and the button through the hole.

I bit my lip as I pushed down his jeans and underwear, freeing his rock hard cock.

"What?" He asked.

I leaned up and kissed him full on the mouth, wrapping my hand around him and jacking him off as I did.

I rubbed the head of his cock against my clit, circling my entrance with the spongy head and coating him in my juices.

"Push in," I whispered against his lips as I lined his cock up with my pussy.

He followed orders, flexing his hips and pushing his stiff length into me.

He didn't stop pushing until he hit the bottom of me, then ground his hips once he did.

"So good," I whispered, my pussy rippling around him, trying to accommodate the suddenness of his thick girth entering me.

"Mig! Answer me!" Jennifer screeched.

I pulled his mouth down to mine, then circled my legs around his hips once again, to urge him on.

He was urged, alright.

He started to thrust into me, hard and deep.

So deep that I saw stars

"Jesus," I breathed, head going back as he hit a certain spot inside of me. "Yes."

His rhythm never changed, and although my eyes were closed, I could tell he was watching me.

I couldn't manage to open them, though.

With each stroke he took into me, the closer and closer I became to an orgasm the likes of which I'd never experienced before.

"The only bathroom I know is in there with you," Jennifer said, right outside the door now.

Mig lost concentration, stopping when he realized how close Jennifer was.

Me, though, all I was was desperate.

I rolled, pushing Mig completely off the bed.

His back hit the carpeted floor with a thump, and he grunted in reaction.

Our connection, however, wasn't lost.

And I used that to my advantage when I started to bounce up and down on his shaft.

I hastily yanked my shirt up and over my breasts, pulling down the cups of my bra so I could reach my nipples beneath.

His hands went to my hips, and grabbed on like I was slowly killing him.

His eyes watched as I pinched and teased my nipples, bringing my breast up to my mouth.

Then, he watched in awe, as I sucked the tip of my nipple into my own mouth.

"Oh, fuck."

I would've smiled, but my mouth was occupied.

He took over then, thrusting up and pulling me down until my orgasm was once more upon me.

And when I went over the peak, throwing my head back in a silent scream, he followed me.

But he wasn't silent.

He yelled.

Loudly.

"Fuck yes!" He bellowed. "Take it all."

I took him all, and then some.

"I can't believe you're in there fucking her when I am in need of a bathroom," Jennifer said in outrage.

I wanted to laugh, but I was doing good to breathe at that moment in time.

My head went down, and I looked at the man beneath me.

"You're bad," he whispered, pinching me on the ass.

I smiled, then removed myself from on top of him.

His cock met his taut belly with a wet smack, and I grinned.

"I'll show you bad," I whispered, turning around so he could see my pussy.

Then I took his cock into my mouth and cleaned him off.

One lick at a time.

***

Hours later, we were both at Chipotle, getting burritos, and I was trying not to drool.

No, not at the sexy beast at my side.

Mig was gorgeous, but he wasn't what had my mouth watering at that moment in time.

No, what had me salivating was the perfect burrito being built for me.

I growled low in my throat when the worker put the first scoop of chicken onto my plate.

"I want double chicken," I said before he could move on to the next item.

He gave me a weird look, and I wanted to laugh.

See, they didn't like it when you fucked with your scoops at Chipotle. They'd try to stiff you scoops if you ordered double chicken up front.

They couldn't give you a smaller scoop, because you already knew what a 'normal' scoop was for them.

So they had to give you two scoops of the chicken, at the perfect amounts that one should get when they asked for a second scoop.

Something I explained to Mig, twenty minutes later, as we were finishing up our meal.

I popped a chip into my mouth, and finally answered the question he'd asked me earlier when we'd sat down.

I'd been too hungry to answer, and he'd thought the entire thing was hilarious.

"Yes, I come here a lot. So I know exactly how to order to get the maximum burrito perfection," I explained.

He nodded sagely.

"I could tell," he smiled, taking a sip of his sweet tea.

The large cup looked small in his hand, and my eyes traveled up said hand to the tattoos on his forearm.

"What does that one mean?" I asked, pointing to the band that circled his lower forearm.

He shrugged. "It was spur of the moment. I got it on a whim. All it means is 'focus.'"

I got that he didn't want to speak about it, so I changed the subject.

"That was nice of Alison to volunteer," I said, looking at Mig across the table.

"Yeah, it was. I'm glad, too. I don't want to spend any more time with her than I have to. I've come to a decision, though. I'll just move in with you, and Jennifer can stay at her own place," he said. "If she needs me other than when I bring her grocery runs, she can call me…or you."

I had a feeling that was as good as it was going to get, so I grabbed onto it with both hands.

"That sounds good," I conceded. "But if it gets to be too bad, you're not going to find me helping her at all."

He nodded, a concerned look on his face. "Hopefully it won't be too bad."

CHAPTER 17

*I like to introduce myself by saying 'it's nice to fucking meet you.'
That way I can weed out the losers that'll get butt hurt over my
language in a timelier manner.
-Mig's secret thoughts*

Annie

He was wrong.

It was worse.

Way worse.

I would never wish Jennifer on my worst enemy.

She was needy. She was whiny. And she was pissy.

Add in the hormones on top of all that, and it was damn near unbearable.

"I'm not going back over there. There's only so much one can take, and I've hit my limit today," I grumbled to myself, stomping across Mig's well-manicured lawn to my non-manicured one. Fortunately for Mig, the house hadn't sold yet.

Not that Mig hadn't offered to mow it.

He had.

But it was my lawn. *I* mowed it.

When I felt like it…and right now I didn't feel like it.

Core, my prospect babysitter, started to wave, but then he saw the look on my face, and decided to ignore the usual welcome he gave me when he saw me.

It was a good thing, too.

I was ready to take the first person I saw off at the knees, and that especially went for Mig and Jennifer.

I swear to God, for someone that didn't like his ex-wife, he sure was treating her as if she was something special.

Like just now.

Jennifer had gone on another crying fit about how bad of a person she was. Instead of setting her straight that she *was* a bad person, Mig sat down next to her, gave me a 'will you please leave' look—a look, I might add, that I'd been getting from him a lot in the past week—and started talking to her about how she needed to calm down because it wasn't good for the baby.

I was about to slam the door to my house when a car pulled up in my driveway.

I stopped and turned, looking at the car as the older officer that'd been the one to tell me my ex was gone, stepped out of his car and held up a hand to me in greeting.

"It's okay, Core," I said, who'd stood the moment the car pulled into the driveway.

Core narrowed his eyes at me, then moved them to Officer Shields.

I held up a hand at him and widened my eyes, causing his lips to kick up in a smirk at my reprimand.

"What can I help you with, Officer Shields?" I asked once he'd reached me.

Officer Shields smiled, and I had to admit, he was devilishly handsome, even if he was a lot older than me.

"I wanted to ask you a few questions about your ex-husband, if you don't mind. There're a few things that have been bothering me, and I wanted you to clear them up," he explained.

My brows rose.

"Sure," I said.

It might be really nice not to have to see or hear Jennifer whine for more than an hour.

"Great, do you want to come to the diner with me? I don't want to make you uncomfortable," he said.

I shrugged. "That's fine. You'll have to take me to work afterwards, though. I have to be at the salon in about an hour and a half."

And that's how I ended up driving away with another man instead of waiting for Mig to call me back over.

A ride I took without my phone so he couldn't reach me.

"Do you know evasive maneuvering that can get us away from my babysitter?" I asked, pointing at Core who'd followed us on his bike.

Officer Shields smiled.

"From what I understand, you've got some bad guys responsible for that scar I can see on the side of your head," he said softly. "So if it makes Konn feel better to have you followed wherever you go, then I'm not going to lose him."

I narrowed my eyes. Konn, aka Mig, aka He-Who-Caters-To-His-Ex-Wife, was on my shit list. And I didn't care about making him 'feel better.'

We didn't speak about what he wanted to talk about on the way there.

We spoke about the weather and how unseasonably cold it was for this time of year.

Normally, in October, it was eighties during the day and sixties at night.

Today it didn't get above sixty-five, and it was going on half past two.

When we walked into the diner, everyone looked up, and eyes started to widen.

Normally, I was with Mig when I came in here, so I was sure it was a shock to see me with a hunky, older man.

One who wasn't, might I add, in his uniform.

"Take a seat anywhere you want, but the further away the better," he said.

I went to the very back of the room and slid into the round table that took up the very back booth.

"What can I get y'all to drink?" The waitress asked.

"Sweet tea," I ordered.

"Coffee…black," Officer Shields said with a small smile.

Once the waitress left, he turned to me and started.

"We went through Ross Autrey's computer to see if we could find any links or lines we could follow, but we came across something interesting, and I wanted to know if you knew about it," he said.

I raised a brow.

"Okay," I said slowly "Sock it to me, Officer Shields."

Officer Shield's grinned. "Call me Byron."

I nodded, and he continued.

"Your ex-husband was living a second life. One that was centered entirely upon you," Byron explained.

I sighed.

Of course he did.

Because why not?

"What did he do?" I asked softly.

"He started accounts in your name. You've got at least six open right now, with him as the co-signer." He handed me some papers, and I felt my eyes widening as I saw the dollar amounts associated with each of the accounts. "And we need your permission to sort through these to determine where the money's originating from."

I nodded. "Of course you have my permission. What all do you need from me?"

"Just consent for now. If we need to go further, we will," he explained.

My stomach clenched as I thought about what all those zeros on that bank statement meant.

"None of that money is mine. I've never seen that many zeros in my life," I told Byron.

Byron nodded. "Me neither. That's pretty impressive."

I agreed.

It was.

Just not how he'd acquired it, since I was sure he was dealing drugs to get that much in the first place.

"Okay. What else did you have questions about?" I asked.

He produced more papers from the front inside pocket of the jacket he was wearing and placed them on the table in front of me.

"Do you know who Liam Cornell is?" He asked.

I blinked.

Then nodded.

"Yes, I do," I confirmed, my stomach knotting in agony at hearing his name.

"He's listed as your ex's employer on his life insurance policy," he started. "But we can't find what 'business' he owns, and we were hoping you could shine some light on him for us."

I didn't want to shine any light on him.

The last time I'd tried to help someone find anything out about Liam Cornell, I'd ended up with a headache the size of Texas, and a radical change in clientele…not that Mig realized that.

Because if he had, he wouldn't be very happy.

But there was no way I was giving Mig one more reason to hate Liam Cornell.

Not if I could help it, anyway.

"The only reason I know the name Liam Cornell is because he used to be a client of mine," I replied. "But he's also who Mig suspects was the reason for this," I said, fingering my still sore part of my face where the wood had connected with my cheek.

"Why does your boyfriend think it was him?" Byron asked.

I sighed. "I'd really like you to talk with Mig about that. He knows a lot more about him, and since my attack, I'm uncomfortable even talking about the man."

Byron nodded sagely.

"The last thing I wanted to talk to you about was your life insurance policy on your ex-husband."

My brows rose, and the skepticism must've showed on my face, because he smiled.

"I can see you didn't know about that, either," he replied.

I shook my head.

"No, I didn't. What kind of life insurance policy was it?" I asked, trying to find the number in the paperwork he'd pushed in front of me.

"Accidental death and dismemberment," he said, pointing at the title of the policy.

But my eyes were caught on the number I'd finally found towards the middle of the page, and my heart had started to pound.

"Three m-million d-dollars?" I stuttered, looking up at Byron.

Byron nodded. "Indeed. As soon as Autrey's death was listed as a murder, the funds were released to be sent to you. But they take around two weeks to a month to arrive, which I'm sure you'll be getting in the mail or electronically, if they set that up with you, very soon."

My mind was a little bit blown.

"Who took the policy out?" I asked in awe.

Byron smiled.

"It was done the day after you were married. He took out a policy on himself with you as a beneficiary and another policy on you, with him as the beneficiary. He pointed to the numbers.

I shook my head.

"That's just…that's just crazy."

***

It wasn't until an hour later, after Byron had dropped me off at my work, that I realized that Mig probably knew about all this money.

There was no way he didn't know.

He'd practically bugged me for every bit of information about my ex-husband. Where he liked to go when he was off work. Why he never had a job. Who his friends were. What his passwords used to be.

You name it, he asked about it.

And he never once said a word about any other bank accounts.

"You forgot to bring your phone," Mig said from the doorway.

I'd known he was there.

In fact, I'd known it was his bike approaching when he was two blocks away.

And now he was standing there, looking perplexed, as if he had no idea why I was so upset. As if he hadn't just dismissed me—again—to cater to Jennifer. He should be thanking me for putting up with Jennifer and her shit!

"I didn't forget a damn thing," I told him, picking up all the bottles of lotion and oil I would be using for this session.

I could hear Mig inhale as if I'd surprised him, but I didn't stay long enough to confirm or deny it.

"You can't just leave without letting me know. I had to go to work, and you were just suddenly gone. I had to call Alison to sit with Jennifer," Mig growled at me.

I looked at him beside me out of my peripheral vision.

"I don't know what I expected when I agreed to help you with this," I said, turning around and pacing to the windows before turning back to explain. "But... what I wasn't expecting was how you've been catering—unnecessarily—to her every whim. I wasn't expecting that when she said jump, you would. I wasn't expecting just how much she'd take advantage of the situation, or how much you'd let her. And I definitely wasn't expecting to be dismissed so often by you. You said it yourself, she's a master manipulator, and she knows exactly what she's doing. But the thing that bothers me most is that you're letting her do it, and it's hurting us in the process."

He sighed and ran his hand through his hair…what little was left of it.

Which was another thing that pissed me off.

Jennifer had made the comment that Mig's hair was getting long and that wasn't the way he normally liked to wear it.

So what does he do?

He fucking cuts it!

That's not to say that I don't like the short hair, because I do, what I don't like is the way she mentions something, and he jumps to do her bidding.

Deciding Mig needed to be put in his place, I opened my mouth to let him have it, but my three thirty client walked in, and he did not look good at all.

"Mr. Gains," I said congenially. "What did you do to yourself this time?"

Mr. Gains, aka 'The Gripper', was an MMA fighter.

He kicked ass all day long, and he got deep tissue massages at least once a week.

"Caught one to the cheek," he laughed pleasantly. "You ready for me?"

He gave Mig an odd, almost excited look, and I couldn't quite decipher what that look meant.

But I didn't stay to examine it for long.

Not when I was ready to get this session over and done with so I could go home or maybe to my sister's.

I thought I might need a little time away from Mig and his inattentiveness.

I patted the table once I got in the room, then set my bottles down on the table beside the bed.

Mr. Gains stripped off his shirt, whipping it off and throwing it down onto the chair across the room.

His pants followed the shirt, but I'd turned around to get my oils ready by that point, and didn't get to look.

Not that Mr. Gains hadn't offered to let me try out the merchandise.

I'd declined.

Mig was kind of hard to get out of your head once he was there.

And Mig was there…in my head…all the goddamn time.

I couldn't get him out of my mind if I tried.

Not that I really wanted to get rid of him…I just wanted him to stop being stupid.

I looked up at Mig who was across the room, and I glared at him.

His eyes narrowed back at me as I worked my hands over my client's back, causing my client to moan.

"My God, your hands are magical," Mr. Gain's said in a low groan.

I smiled devilishly at Mig, moving my hands more sensually.

I usually didn't notice how 'sensual' or 'not sensual' I did things when I massaged.

Truly, to me, this was a job.

It was my job to make this man's back feel better, and his massive amount of muscles wouldn't normally have been that big of a deal.

But Mig and his narrowed eyes were across the room, watching, and I was pissed at him.

So what did I do?

Something stupid.

I massaged Mr. Gain's like I was making love to his body with my hands.

And Mig saw every single bit of the show.

He stayed that way, watching me work, with fisted hands.

And if I'd been smart, I would've stopped.

But I didn't.

And Mig watched the entire show with a very pissed off expression on his face.

And only when I was done did he leave, and I realized that just maybe I shouldn't have poked that particular sleeping bear.

CHAPTER 18

Missing: Beard. Last seen: Between my thighs.
-T-shirt

Mig

"What are you doing here?" The Gripper, also known as 'Mr. Gains' asked.

I ignored him, walking into the main room of Uncertain Principles, the gym that Casten owned.

Casten was an ambitious guy.

He owned his own bounty hunter business, which was doing pretty well for him.

And he also owned the one and only fighter gym in Uncertain, which also happened to be the only fighter gym in the entire area.

"It's time," I said, walking over to the bench.

I think I rendered Adam speechless, because he didn't say a word as he watched me walk away.

CeeCee, Casten's sister, came out of the office with a smile on her face.

"What are you doing here, Mig?" CeeCee asked.

I started to strip my cut off, followed shortly by my shirt.

"It's time," I repeated for her.

CeeCee looked at me like I'd grown a second head.

"You told me two years ago when I met you that you'd never fight again. What's different about today?" She asked.

I liked CeeCee.

She was cute, sweet, and an overall awesome woman.

See, here's the thing, Adam Gains knows exactly who I am.

I work out here just like the rest of our brothers.

But I don't fight.

Ever.

I shadow boxed. I did everything any other fighter would do in their workout routine…except fighting an actual person.

Give me a bag, and I was happy.

Give me a person, and it wasn't happening.

Until today.

Until I watched my woman rub her hands all over Adam fucking *Gains*.

And he knew the moment he walked in the door that Annie was mine.

Knew it, and I'd bet he's probably known it for a while.

He's been looking for a way to get me to fight him, and it looks like today was his day—he was going to get his wish.

Watching Annie rub her hands all over him like he was her lover, was the straw that broke the proverbial camel's back.

I turned around as I emptied my pockets onto the bench that ran along the outside wall of the gym.

The last thing I took off was my gun, which I handed to Casten as he walked through the door with a bag of what appeared to be fast food for him and CeeCee.

"Here, hold this," I ordered, handing the gun to him.

He took it without a word, hooking the clip onto his jeans and continuing walking as if I hadn't stopped him at all.

Finally, I turned to Adam.

Adam smiled.

"It's not like I had any control over how she massaged me today. I was a perfect gentleman," Adam said.

I narrowed my eyes.

"Yep, you sure were. But you also didn't leave when you knew I wanted you to," I said tightly.

Adam laughed.

"I knew that if I could piss you off enough, you might spar with me," he said tauntingly.

I narrowed my eyes.

"You know I don't fight anymore," I countered stonily.

Adam smiled.

"Yeah, but you're pissed, aren't you? Want to plant your hand in my face," Adam goaded.

My fists clenched.

I *did* want to plant my fist in his face—and I would.

And I did want to beat the shit out of him.

But I hadn't fought in a ring in well over ten years.

Adam was good.

But he didn't stand a chance against me, although he'd tried to prove otherwise once before, and I'd shut him down, not giving him the fight he wanted.

"I was just doing you a favor, anyhow. She's lost a lot of customers; that's why I started coming once or twice a week instead of every other week," Adam said, smiling.

He slipped his hands into fingerless gloves, watching me, assessing my face, trying to gauge my reaction.

Outwardly I showed no reaction at all, but on the inside, I was stunned.

I hadn't realized that Annie's business had been affected by all of this.

Just how many customers had she lost?

A few?

A lot?

And why hadn't she told me?

Now that I knew, however, I would be able to figure out a way to help her.

And it sickened me that my rash act of confronting Liam Cornell at Annie's salon had made her feel any recourse from that situation at all.

I sat on the bench and slowly started to unlace my boots, taking the time to collect myself as I did it.

The first rule of fighting was not to let anger play a part in your decision to fight.

And that was what Adam had been trying to accomplish.

Once my boots and socks were off, I stood up and stretched my arms up high above my head.

My spine cracked as it lengthened, and I wanted to laugh when CeeCee made a gagging sound.

She hated it when people popped their knuckles or their backs, and made no secret of her opinions.

The door jingled again, causing me to glance in its direction out of habit.

I wasn't at all surprised to see Peek, Ridley, Wolf and Griffin coming through the door, either.

The office that Griffin, Wolf and I shared was located just down the street, so it wouldn't have been that hard for them to get here.

Peek and Ridley, though, had been out of town.

Vaguely I wondered why and when they got back, but chose not to question it until I was done with my fight.

It shouldn't take long.

"Who's officiating?" Adam asked as I finally moved to the cage.

It wasn't really a cage.

It was more like a ring but surrounded in netting.

It was there as a visual aid and it didn't really serve any other purpose.

"No official. First one to pass out loses," I told him, causing him to blink in surprise.

"Okay," Adam agreed a little too eagerly.

That was a second stupid thing he'd done.

Adam was pretty smart, but he let his emotions get the best of him.

I knew he was excited to fight me.

He wasn't, however, excited to know we were only going one round.

"How is that going to accomplish anything?" Adam asked in confusion.

"Don't worry, I'm going to let you get a good 20 seconds in before I knock you out," I taunted.

He narrowed his eyes on me, and I heard an amused chuckle from behind me.

Casten.

He knew this would be my fight.

I would control every aspect of it.

Adam would be along for the ride, so to speak.

"Fine," Adam said, holding out his hands.

I punched them, taking a deep breath, before I launched right in to my attack.

See, that's the thing about me.

People, or other fighters, expected a big man like me to be slow.

I probably had fifty pounds on Adam.

Normally, we'd be in different weight classes, but I knew Adam could take a punch.

He'd been trained by Casten.

But he'd never had to fight for his life.

Deep down, Adam was basically a good guy, he just needed to learn to control his mouth better.

And to stay away from my woman, I thought darkly.

I switched off those thoughts and cast my mind back to a place it hadn't been in well over ten years—since that last summer when I was twenty and spent a week with my father.

It'd also been the very last lesson he'd ever given me.

And I remembered every single bit of it.

I'd taken that knowledge into the Air Force with me.

I'd honed my body into the machine that my father had started sculpting, and I'd only gotten bigger, stronger and more solid since.

Something I was about to prove to Adam.

See, the real the reason I wouldn't spar with Adam wasn't because I didn't want to—it was because I *did*.

In a few minutes, every man here would learn who was the real fighter in the room.

But it was never good to reveal your hand too early, because if you ever had to use the skills that I possessed, then you weren't in a good place.

If Adam knew how good I was he'd bug me incessantly until I helped to train him.

Adam was a good fighter, and part of the reason why was that he was not only religious about his training, but he also had an unquenchable thirst for knowledge about the sport.

He wanted to better himself, and the only way to do that, he had to fight someone better than him.

Adam swung his left fist, pulling it at the last second so it glanced off my jaw instead of taking me at the temple.

I smiled.

He'd have never connected, but he didn't know that.

Rule Number One of Konn Fight School: Don't pull your punches.

You fight to survive. You do what you have to do to get your opponent down on the ground, and you don't stick around to see how he fared.

I retaliated with a right hook to Adam's lower belly, causing him to lean forward slightly.

"Guard!" Casten bellowed.

I wanted to laugh.

Adam wouldn't be fast enough. Nice try, though, coach.

Instead of hitting him with the fist to the face that he would be expecting, I swept my right foot out, and tripped him.

Adam stumbled but didn't go down.

But it was enough to get him off balance, and I used that to my advantage.

The next five minutes I used to show him just how important it was to guard.

I bobbed, swooped, ducked, jabbed and just generally beat the crap out of Adam.

Not enough to knock him out, but he did start losing steam.

Fast.

He was good, I'd give him that. But he wasn't at my level, and it was likely that he never would be.

I wasn't being conceited, it was just obvious that I was better than him.

Adam was definitely good, but I'd just had more...*experience*. My skills were ingrained in me from years of my father's lessons, my time in the military and now the DEA.

You can learn the motions, use them, and live by them.

But you're not a killer until you've watched the life drain out of another human being's eyes.

Knowing that you were responsible for putting that look there.

And when I fought, I was willing to kill if I had to.

Adam, however, wasn't.

He was moving inefficiently, exhausting himself and just going through the motions now.

Something I saw him realize just seconds later.

"You're just playing with me, aren't you?" He breathed through a gasping breath.

I grinned.

"You wanted it, you got it."

He swung a slow punch at my kidney, and I blocked and turned, bringing his back to my front without effort.

I could see the moment he realized he was defeated.

But instead of knocking him out, I followed the move up with a nerve strike to his neck, bringing him down to his knees.

Although he'd be awake and aware, he wouldn't be able to move his legs properly for about a half-hour or so.

"Win," I said to him.

He hung his head.

"Win," he confirmed.

The gym was silent as I walked out of the ring to my belongings.

Without a word I dressed, only stopping to grab my gun from Casten before I was out the door and heading to work since it was probably the best place for me right now.

At least until I shook off this noxious attitude and was able to talk to Annie with some semblance of control.

Lani Lynn Vale

CHAPTER 19

*There's a fine line to how much stupidity I can take before it
exceeds the limit of my medication. And unfortunately for you, you
just crossed it.
-Mig to a perp*

Annie

I don't know what I expected of Mig when I walked into my house later
that evening.

But it wasn't the man I got.

"Have you had dinner yet?" I asked softly, eying the way he lounged on
the couch with a wariness that didn't bode well for our evening.

"No," he rumbled low in his throat.

I swallowed thickly, very aware of the way he was looking at me like *I*
was dinner.

"I'm making steak and mashed potatoes. It's all I have."

I'd been meaning to go to the store for the past couple of days, but I'd
been avoiding it since I knew that it would inevitably turn into an errand
for Jennifer.

And I wasn't buying her groceries. There was only so much waiting on
and catering to her that I could stomach, and I had surpassed my limit
now.

She was totally taking advantage of us and milking her situation for all it
was worth.

So, Jennifer could suck it.

And I would've almost believed that I would do anything for her if she truly needed it, because I couldn't stop thinking about the innocent life she was carrying.

The baby who had no say in who her parents were or how they behaved.

Suddenly, it all became so very real.

What was I to Mig?

Was I supposed to be his girlfriend?

Could I be the kind of girlfriend who takes care of her man's baby from another woman?

What if I wanted kids of my own?

"Mig?" I asked, shutting the fridge softly and turning around.

He looked up from the couch, and it was then I saw the shiner on his eye.

"What happened to your face?" I asked in alarm.

He grinned.

"Just a little bit of release. You got me all riled up, and I didn't want to take it out on you when I got here, so I burned it all off at the gym," he mumbled, returning his gaze to the TV.

That move clearly shut down any further questioning about the shiner, so I decided to broach the other topic.

"What are you going to do once the baby gets here?" I asked softly.

He shrugged.

"I figured I'd take him or her with me to work when I could. When I can't, I'll take the baby to daycare," he mumbled, not bothering to look away from the screen.

I blinked.

Then walked around the couch to sit on the coffee table, effectively cutting off his view of the TV.

"Mig," I hesitated when his eyes finally met mine. His eye looked awful. "A baby can't go to daycare until they're at least six weeks old."

His brows furrowed.

"Since when?" He asked.

I snorted.

"Since always," I challenged.

He dropped the TV changer onto the couch beside him, then lifted his arms to work his hands into his hair.

"I never really thought about it, I guess. I'd always thought Jennifer would be there to take care of the baby. Since she went on bed rest, I've done a lot of avoiding, rather than thinking, about the consequences of taking the baby from Jennifer." He looked at me finally. "I haven't even told my family. They never even knew I was married."

My brows rose, and I stood up, offering him my hand.

"Then let's go tell them," I said. "But first we need to make a quick stop. I need to pick up a few things."

He stopped me before I could get more than two steps away from him.

"My family lives nearly ten hours from here," he told me.

I blinked, then took a seat back where I was sitting before.

"Well then, maybe we should plan that for this weekend, eh?" I teased.

He didn't smile.

"When were you going to tell me you've lost customers because of Cornell?" He growled.

My eyes widened.

"How do you know that?" I asked warily.

I'd never seen Mig like this.

Never seen him quite so…aggressive.

It wasn't to say that I didn't find him hot, because he was.

But I'd also never seen him so pissed off at me before.

I hadn't done anything!

He had enough on his plate dealing with Jennifer to take on something this petty. It was just a couple of clients!

"Annie," Mig sat up on the couch.

This put my legs in between his, and his face only inches from mine.

And suddenly I was not thinking about my business anymore.

I was thinking about how good he smelled.

I thought it might be his deodorant, because I'd never seen him put on anything other than that since he moved in my to home.

Every morning his routine was the same.

Get up before the sun even rose. Go for a run. Eat some oatmeal. Shower. If I was awake, he'd fuck me, and if I wasn't, he'd just get dressed. And he always gave me a kiss before he left for the day.

And during those times that I did get used thoroughly, he'd get dressed while I watched, barely able to move.

He always slipped his underwear on first, followed by his pants, socks, shoes, shirt and then lastly he'd swipe on some deodorant.

I never once saw him put any cologne on.

So there I was, contemplating making his deodorant into a candle when he grabbed my face.

"Are you even listening to me?" He asked sharply.

My lips were smashed together, and I looked at him while I spoke in what sounded mostly like gibberish through my squashed lips.

"Oo mell ood," I told him.

He eased up on my face, cupping my ears instead, and asked, "What?"

"I said you smell good," I repeated.

He blinked.

"What?"

"You." I poked him with accusation. "Smell." Poke. "Good."

His lips twitched.

"So we're done talking about your customers?" He asked.

I shrugged. "There's not really much to say here. Liam Cornwell is bad mouthing me around town. My business has slowed down, yes, but not enough to where I'm worried yet. I've lost maybe six clients total. But I've already replaced those six clients with new ones, so it's all good."

"How do you know it's Liam?" He asked curiously.

"My clients called and told me," I explained.

He nodded, lifting both of his roughened hands to run them down his handsome face.

"I'm looking for him, I swear," he said, finally lifting his head and pinning me with his gaze. "He won't be able to do this much longer. He's burning through his resources fast, and it's only a matter of time before he gets cocky and fucks up."

I leaned forward until my head was resting on his shoulder.

His shoulder was like a ball of solid muscle.

It felt like I was resting my forehead against a rock.

A very sexy rock, but a rock nonetheless.

"I'm not worried, Mig. I know you'll take care of this," I whispered.

He wrapped his arms around me, pulling me into his warm embrace.

"You don't deserve to deal with this shit," he muttered.

I tipped my head back until my boobs were resting on his forearms.

"Mig, shit happens in life, and we deal. This isn't anyone but Liam Connell's fault, so stop blaming yourself." I informed him.

He grinned, his straight white teeth standing out starkly against his tanned face.

His shaved hair looked a little better today than it had the day before, and I wanted to rub my hands all along the top of his head.

I refrained, though.

Barely.

"I'll take that under advisement," he muttered, his gaze moving down to my lips.

I parted them slightly, and nearly laughed when he inhaled sharply.

"I'm hungry," he lied.

"Yeah?" I asked, leaning forward until my mouth was only millimeters from his.

"Yeah," he confirmed.

Then his lips were on mine.

Our hands tangled as we each reached for the other's shirt.

His was first, followed immediately by mine.

Next to go was my bra. His pants. My shoes. His underwear. And finally my pants and underwear, all in one fell swoop.

He pulled me onto his lap, the shaft of his hard cock nestled in the seam of my pussy, as we both started to slowly move our hips.

My breasts were pressed tight to his chest, the fine hairs tickling my nipples and stimulating them.

"You're almost as good as dinner, I suppose," he rumbled, his hand going to my hair to expose my throat fully to him.

His lips skimmed up the side of my throat, and I laughed breathlessly.

"Almost?" I asked, sitting forward and reaching behind me to guide his cock to my entrance.

He helped me by holding his cock as I slowly slid down his length.

Filled completely with him his hand went to my ass my body adjusted to his girth.

I started to move, sliding all the way up the length of him to the very tip before dropping slowly back down

His thumb ventured down to sweep across my entrance, and my body hummed in anticipation.

He'd tried this once before, and he'd caught the hesitancy on my face, so he didn't take it very far.

This time, though, he let his thumb gather the wetness around my stretched entrance, then he drug it up to the rosette of my ass and slowly started to massage there.

My nipples pebbled, and I leaned my head forward until it rested on his shoulder.

My arms encircled his neck, and I kept up the pace sliding up and back down on him.

Not too fast, but not slow.

Just right for now, allowing him to work without trying to keep up with my jostling movements.

I gasped when he finally slipped his thumb inside, my eyes squeezing tightly shut as sparks of pure pleasure burst through me.

Who knew that having a thumb in your ass felt as good as it did?

And I'm not talking a little bit of good, I'm talking about a lot of good.

I couldn't decide which feeling to focus on.

The way his thumb felt, teasing me in a way that I'd never been teased before, or the way his huge, hard cock filled me perfectly, dragging across that spot inside of me that only he had been able to reach.

In the end, it didn't matter what I focused on.

I was on fire for him and barreling toward a massive orgasm.

He had three fingers inside of me when I came, and I came so hard that I screamed.

Loudly.

"Mig!"

He growled as my hips slowed, taking over the movements with both of his hands on my hips. controlling the movement for his pleasure now.

He quickly moved me along his length and slammed me down, three more times before he exploded inside of me.

Short, strong bursts of his semen poured inside my pussy, making me momentarily wish that I wasn't on birth control.

That his seed would take root.

I shook those thoughts away, and I focused on the present.

Didn't need them any time soon, either.

Which was why, instead of focusing on what could be, I focused on what we had now.

"Do you even have any of the things you'll need for the baby?" I asked him, turning my head to study his profile.

His eyes were closed, and he was breathing hard.

Contentment started to slowly seep into my limbs.

I licked my lips, but Mig's next words had panic rising in my throat.

"No. I don't have anything. What do they need? Diapers and clothes?" He asked, sounding tired.

I blinked, sitting up to stare at him.

"You're kidding, right?" I asked carefully.

He blinked. "What do you mean?"

I stood up, immediately rethinking how awesome it was to have sex without a condom.

Seriously, sex was messy business.

Who knew?

CHAPTER 20

*How interesting would life be if our thoughts appeared in bubbles
over our heads?
-Annie's secret thoughts*

Mig

"I don't want to register for it. I just want to buy the shit that you think
we need and leave," I muttered.

Annie shot me an annoyed look.

"People are going to want to buy you things, and if you don't have a
registry, they won't know what you need," she explained slowly, picking
up a huge package of diapers.

I blinked. "Do we really need all of that right now?" I asked.

She didn't bother to answer; instead, moving to put a huge box of wipes
into the cart, followed by smaller tubs and packages of the same.

The more she continued to add to the cart, the more I could see the
dollars adding up.

"Here, which one?" She asked, pointing to the two car seats directly in
front of her.

"What's wrong with that one?" I asked, pointing to the cheaper one.

"That one is made for bigger kids. This one is for a newborn," she
indicated.

I pointed to the cheaper one.

"That one is fine," I said.

She chose the teal-colored one that I had *not* pointed at.

"Will you go get another cart? We're going to need at least two, if not three," she said.

Reluctantly, I walked away in a hurry, worried that if I took too long, she'd buy the whole fuckin' section.

I got looks as I exited the baby section, and I couldn't wait to see people's faces when I had an actual baby in my arms.

Big ass biker and a tiny baby.

That was going to be fun.

After grabbing the cart, I hurried back to the baby section, taking a short-cut through the big kid section.

I picked up a monkey with long arms, surveying it on the way back to Annie.

I'd just rounded the corner of the aisle where she'd been when I left, only to find it empty.

The next one was empty as well.

By the time I hit up the third aisle, my heart started to pound.

And when I'd made an entire circuit of the baby department, I called for her.

"Annie!"

Customers looked at me, but I didn't care that I'd just yelled bringing everyone's attention my way.

I was more worried that I'd been stupid and left her alone when I knew she shouldn't be left alone.

"Annie!" I called again.

An elderly woman snapped at me.

"Is she the pretty girl in the red shirt?" She asked.

I nodded. "Yes, did you see where she went?"

She pointed in the direction of the restrooms that were at the very back of the store.

"She went that way, left her cart right there," she indicated where the cart was parked.

I thanked her and moved towards the bathroom.

I didn't stop at the door, either.

I barged right in, and what I saw had me seeing red.

"What happened?" I demanded.

She had a wad of toilet paper covering her mouth that was quickly saturating with blood.

She pulled the rag away from her mouth.

"Some guy shoved me from behind, and I fell, hitting my lip on the rack before I went down," she explained. "I don't think he meant to."

I doubted that.

Bumping into her, I could see. Full out pushing her to her hands and knees, I couldn't.

The cut was on the inside of her mouth, making me realize that it could've been worse than it was.

"What'd he look like?" I asked her.

She shook her head.

"I don't know. I only saw his gray shoes as he walked away. I guess I'm just lucky he didn't take the opportunity to steal my purse that was sitting right there in the cart," she explained, wincing slightly when she pulled her lip tight over her teeth. "It was all messed up like he started to look through it for my wallet."

Thirty minutes later, we left Target with twenty percent off our entire purchase since I'd kicked up one hell of a fuss over the fact that their entire fucking security system had conveniently gone down.

I didn't take the discount.

Annie did.

Which, in turn, meant I was still mad, just keeping a tight lid on it until I could get home and talk to the club to see what we were going to do about this.

"I'm going to try to…" I started to say, but the sight of lights up ahead near my house shut me down before I finished that thought.

"What the fuck?" I asked as I swung into Annie's driveway.

The first person I saw was Wolf, who was standing in the middle of Annie's yard with a grim look on his face.

I got out, slamming the truck's door, and walked over to him.

"What happened?" I asked, looking at my house.

"Alison called the cops because she kept hearing someone knocking on the backdoor," Wolf explained. "When they got here, they saw what looked to be blood on the back porch, but was actually ketchup…a lot of it…smeared all over the back porch, almost like someone had rolled around in it."

My teeth started to grind together.

"Did you check the feed?" I asked.

Wolf nodded. "It's out. Your line was cut from the pole, but your generator kicked on, not even letting Alison see anything more than a flicker, so she didn't know to call."

I had a generator that had a four second delay.

When power was lost, it kicked on, but only certain things worked.

Like the fridge, the lights and the AC.

Small things, such as the security system, weren't hooked up to it.

Something that only a professional would know.

My generator was hard to miss.

It stuck out like a sore thumb right to the side of the front of my house.

I got asked all the time by people that didn't know me what it was, and I always told them that's where I put my trashcans.

Although half right, it wasn't solely for that purpose.

"We were at Target tonight and someone pushed Annie, made her fall and hit the rack of clothes in front of her," I told him. "When I went to see the camera feed to see what exactly happened, they couldn't tell me because their security system had been turned off for a total of eight minutes, during which time, Annie took her fall."

Wolf slowly turned to look at me.

"Convenient."

I nodded.

It was.

Too convenient.

"I think it's time to call my old man. See what his boys can find," I said. "I've tried to do it myself, but this guy has the connections required to hide himself, and I think he's finally decided to stop playing with me and do some real harm."

And it was time for me to hire someone to watch over Annie and, I guess, Jennifer.

I didn't think Jennifer would be a target, mostly because she was the reason this had all started.

But I was proved wrong tonight, and had she been alone, I was sure I would be staring at an empty house right now instead of one that contained a pissed off Jennifer.

"That may be the best idea right now," Wolf said.

"What's your father going to do that you can't?" Annie questioned softly from behind me.

I turned to her, seeing that she was holding a hand full of bags.

"My father has bodyguards that are very loyal to him and the Konn name," I said. "And if he tells them to, which I know he will once he realizes that there's a baby coming, they'll watch over y'all until she has the baby so I can put my full attention into finding this son of a bitch."

Her eyes widened. "You're going to stick me with Jennifer?"

She sounded so appalled at the idea that I laughed.

"It'll be for just a few days, a week tops," I tried.

She narrowed her eyes.

"I'd rather be stuck in prison with half my leg chewed off by rats or even share the jail cell with a large woman named Bertha who has a crush on me," she said stubbornly.

"There is another option," I said.

She lit up at the possibility.

"Anything. Absolutely anything."

I grinned.

"I'll remember you said that."

CHAPTER 21

There's want, and then there's need. Two very different emotions.
One is a short-lived desire, and the other is a permanent passion.
You're the latter on both counts. Forever and always.
-Text from Mig to Annie

Annie

He can't protect you forever. I proved that today. I could've shot you,
and he would've gotten back in time to watch you bleed to death.

I read the note for a second time, then a third, as I tried to control my pounding heart.

I wasn't dead.

He hadn't killed me.

Mig had been there.

Had scared him off.

I was *okay!*

I shoved the note back into my purse when I heard Mig's steps on the front walk.

He'd gone to check in with Jennifer since we'd be leaving soon.

And I assumed he was letting her know so she didn't worry, or whatever, since we were leaving before her.

Needless to say, Jennifer and I would never be friends

I resented her too much.

I hated the way she treated Mig.

Hated the way she whined about her pitiful life.

Hated that she how she pulled the pregnancy card to get exactly what she wanted.

And to be honest, these two weeks that were almost over couldn't end fast enough.

"Hey," I said to Mig once he opened the door. "How'd she take it?"

Mig grimaced. "Bad. She doesn't like Alison."

I laughed.

Alison was one of the easiest people in the world to get along with.

"And I'm going to have Casten bring her up. She won't be staying with you or my mom, but she'll be in the guest house with her own maid. It'll be like she's not even there," he said.

He'd told me of this possibility, and I was fine with it.

I didn't want Jennifer too far away from Mig.

I knew that their baby would be born at any second, and I didn't want Mig to miss a thing.

"Alright then, I'm ready when you are," I said, holding my bag out to him.

He took it.

"Can Casten bring that one up with him when he comes?" He asked.

I nodded. "Make sure he doesn't forget Katy. She'd be mad at you."

Katy looked up at me from her perch on the couch.

Katy was like a cat in a lot of ways.

She didn't like anybody but me, and she only tolerated Mig.

She hated to get wet, didn't like getting dirty and preferred not to lay on the floor.

She liked to be left alone, and it was very rare that she would seek attention.

She'd just now gotten to the point where she didn't get up and leave when Mig was in the room.

If it were any other person, and you wouldn't see her at all.

I couldn't wait to see how she reacted to Casten bringing her in a car over three hundred miles.

It would be fun times, indeed!

Mig rolled his eyes. "He's already got the 'Hoe cleaned out for Katy's cage and all her numerous belongings."

He looked pointedly at the doggie pillow.

"What?" I asked in affront.

"I've never in my life seen a dog need a pillow for less than a week of vacation. What's wrong with bringing her food dishes, food, and leash?" Mig asked.

I snorted. "You've obviously never owned a pet before. You have to give them what they want to make them comfortable since they'll be in a new place."

He blinked. "It's a dog, not a child."

I shrugged. "Same thing to me."

I vaguely heard him mutter something close sounding to 'not the same thing at all' but chose not to acknowledge it.

I followed behind him as he led me out to his bike.

"And he's going to bring my other suitcase, right?" I asked.

Mig nodded but didn't turn around.

"And what about the car seat and the baby bag—just in case?" I continued.

It wouldn't do to not be prepared.

I'd done all the hard parts: unpacking everything from the bags, washing all the clothes, and getting the diaper bag stocked with the essentials according to my mom's instructions.

I was ready to roll, so to speak.

Now all we needed was the baby.

I felt like I was looking in from the outside, though.

Once he or she was here, what would I do?

Would he ask me to help? Would he ask me to leave and give him some time?

He'd made an off the wall comment about asking his mother to come help when the baby arrived, but he hasn't said another word about it.

Now I was left wondering.

And I hated being in the dark.

"Can we stop by my parent's place before we go? I want to pick up something she made for me," I said.

My mother had called saying she'd had a dream about me last night, and that she'd made me some cookies because she couldn't sleep after waking up from her nightmare.

So, being the good daughter that I was, I'd go reassure her and take my cookies…because who would pass up fresh-baked cookies from their mom?

"Your parents live close to your sister, right?" He asked as he turned around, leaning against the bike.

He looked so sexy.

The morning rays of sunshine were filtering through a large, white, fluffy cloud that was passing in front of the sun.

Him leaning against his bike, wearing his Uncertain Saints MC cut, dark washed jeans and black boots, in the soft morning sunlight gave him an almost sleepy, sexy glow. It made him look like the sexiest man alive.

I had to resist the urge to lick my lips.

"Yeah, they about two minutes from Tasha," I confirmed.

He nodded, holding out his hand for me.

"Your dad going to be home?" He asked once I placed my hand in his.

I shrugged. "Maybe…maybe not. He does a lot of fishing now that he's retired. And it's a pretty nice day out today. I highly doubt that he would. My mom will be though."

He grinned.

"Moms like me," he teased.

I had no doubt that they did.

My mom was a woman after all, and although she was a *married* woman, she wasn't blind and could certainly appreciate the sight of a hot guy just as well as a single woman.

"What woman doesn't like you?" I asked.

He took the only bag that he'd allowed me to carry with us and shoved it unceremoniously into one of the huge saddle bags that had showed up on his bike this morning.

I had to laugh when he barely got it to close.

He shot me a disgruntled look.

And I pretended to zip my mouth shut and throw away the key.

"Funny, but I don't believe for a second that you'll really zip it," he grumbled.

Mig was in a weird mood.

It upset him every time he looked at me and saw my mouth swollen from my fall.

He was also upset that his ex-wife called him four times—*four times*—during the night because she was 'scared,' even though she knew that Casten was right there in the next room.

He looked tired, even with his sunglasses on.

"Well, let's go then," he said, straddling the bike.

I mounted behind him, making the comment that he needed to scooch his booty forward so I could sit comfortably behind him.

"There's a seat back there," he said.

I looped my arms around his belly and leaned my head against his back once I had my helmet on, then nodded.

"I know. But I like clinging to you like a monkey," I teased.

He didn't say anything to that, and I was wondering if it was a good thing or a bad thing.

But then he started the bike, I saw a smile on his face as he turned to check behind him before pulling out of the driveway.

I waved at Jennifer, who was on the front porch watching us.

She scowled at me, and I clung to Mig tighter, thankful that it was not me watching from the front porch this time.

The ride to my mother's was quick, and I was surprised to see my mom and sister on the front porch, drinking a cup of coffee.

I dismounted before Mig could, then tugged my helmet off as I hurried up the sidewalk.

"Those are my cookies!" I yelled at my betraying sister.

My sister smiled and took another bite of the cookie.

I snatched it away, shoving it in my mouth as I ran inside.

Tasha was quick on my heels, and I knew she'd catch up to me any moment.

She had longer legs than I did, so I had to resort to drastic measures.

Which was why I slammed the door in her face, then locked it.

She pounded on the door for long seconds before it abruptly stopped.

I hurried to the garage door and locked it, too.

Tasha showed up once I threw the dead bolt.

Her eyes narrowed, and I grinned.

She looked over to the window that was open on the opposite side of the room, and I took off at the same time she did.

She only had to run around the house.

I had to run down a hallway, scoot around the bar, and then go down another hallway to get to the open window.

It was a weird set up, and I blamed my parents for buying such a stupid house.

Knowing when to throw in the towel, I ran to the kitchen and grabbed my plate of cookies, laughing when I heard my sister curse as she fell to her hands and knees on the opposite side of the house.

I walked calmly through the family room and then walked back outside with my plate of cookies in one hand and a bottle of Fanta in the other.

My dad drank Fanta.

It wasn't my favorite, but it was what they had.

So I took it.

I gracefully took the seat that my sister had been previously occupying.

I saw my sister's coffee and helped myself to a large gulp before shoving half a cookie in my mouth.

Then, for good measure, I licked every single one of the seven cookies on the plate, making sure to leave a generous amount of spit on them, before I took another gulp of coffee.

Only then did I look up to see my sister, mother and Mig watching me like I was crazy.

"What?" I asked.

Mig's lips twitched before giving in to the first smile I'd seen on his face today.

"That's just disgusting," Tasha grumbled, sitting down on the steps next to where Mig was standing.

"Mom, did you meet Mig?" I asked around a mouthful of cookie.

My mother nodded.

"Yes, I did," she said.

My mother was all of five feet tall and curvy.

Today, she looked like she hadn't bothered to finish getting dressed.

Her hair was still up in the bun that she normally slept in every night.

She was still wearing her nightgown, along with a robe, and her favorite pair of house slippers.

"Why aren't you dressed? It's nearly ten in the morning," I asked.

My mother shrugged.

"I was going to go take a nap since your father will be gone fishing all day. You said you weren't sure if you would be able to make it before you left, so I didn't see any reason to get dressed," she said. "Then your sister came over to tell me you fell and banged up your face. So, here I am wondering why my daughter did not tell me what happened to her when I was on the phone telling her about a nightmare I had about her getting hurt?"

"Oops," I said, shoving a cookie into my mouth. "And how does Tasha know anyway? I didn't tell her."

Tasha smiled deviously. "I have a new friend."

I raised a brow at her.

"Who?" I asked.

She pulled out her phone and showed me a picture of Casten.

My mouth dropped open.

"No!" I said loudly. "You can't have him, he's mine."

Tasha narrowed her eyes.

"You have Mig; you can't have Casten, too," she said stubbornly.

"But he belongs to Mig! You'll ruin him, and Mig will lose his best friend!" I said.

I wasn't exactly sure if that was true, but it sounded good.

Tasha did have a way of burning people out, though.

She was fun and flirty, but she was also flighty and definitely the love 'em and leave 'em type.

It really wasn't because she wanted to break innocent men's hearts but because she seriously couldn't help it.

She had no control over how awesome she was, and Tasha got bored easily.

If you couldn't constantly keep her entertained, which was damn near impossible, she'd just go find something—or someone—else to entertain her.

Which explained why she was currently in nursing school.

She didn't really want to be a nurse, she just needed the challenge.

And Casten was probably giving her exactly what she wanted: a challenge.

"Did he call you?" I asked curiously.

Tasha shook her head. "No. I texted him like I do every night. That's the only way I get information about you."

That was true.

I tried to protect my family from the drama was going on around me. They didn't need to be worried about me, too.

"Casten's not going to get hurt," Mig said drolly. "He's a big boy."

I wanted to laugh.

Mig had *no* idea.

Well, at least it would be fun to watch.

"These are really good cookies, mom. Thank you for making them," I said, taking another bite of cookie.

They were chocolate chip, made with big chocolate chunks instead of chips.

"You're welcome, *mi hija*," my mother said. "Don't think that you're off the hook, though."

Uh-oh.

If my Puerto Rican mommy was using Spanish, she was upset.

When we were little, my father had wanted to teach us Spanish, since it was their primary language, but my mother had been adamantly opposed to it.

'We're in America. We speak English.'

My father still spoke Spanish whenever the hell he felt like it, but he didn't push the issue with my mother.

I never quite figured out what exactly the trigger was that caused her to revert back to Spanish. Usually, it was when she was extremely stressed, but that wasn't the only time she did it.

I just knew that if mom was speaking Spanish, she was pissed, worried, excited or a crazy combination of those feelings.

Therefore, I did what I did best.

I ran away.

"Gotta go, mom!" I said, hopping to my feet. "Mig and I have a lot of miles to put in before we get to Alabama."

Mig, sensing there was something amiss, held his hand out to my mother.

"It was nice to meet you, and I'll take you up on that dinner next week," he said, shaking the hand my mother offered him.

Dinner was a family affair.

Always.

So for my mother to invite Mig, without knowing him for more than five minutes, was huge.

Plus, it also didn't hurt that my mother knew I had a crush on my next-door neighbor.

She'd also been there the day I saw Mig ride into town on his Harley.

She never forgot a face, and her mind was like steel trap.

She never forgot anything she was told.

And clearly she had not forgotten my drunken confession about why I wanted to divorce Ross.

I want a man like Mig. A man that makes my heart pound. A man that would protect me with his life. Who won't ever let me go. And if I say I want him to, he'll fight for me.

And, what I said to her still held true today.

Hopefully I had that, because I don't think I could let Mig go now even if I tried.

CHAPTER 22

I'd rather live life as an honest sinner than a lying, fuckwad hypocrite.
-Mig's secret thoughts

Annie

I furiously tapped Mig's shoulder, pointing to the side of the road where I wanted him to stop.

He dutifully pulled over, without a complaint, and turned the bike off.

"What are we doing?" Mig asked.

I pointed to the Louisiana/Alabama state line.

"There," I indicated the big sign.

He pulled over, stopping right over the state line.

Then, with a huge smile on my face, I got off his bike and walked back to the sign that distinguished the area in front of me as the spot I was looking for.

Then I hopped over a foot to my right.

"Did you see?" I asked him loudly.

He was studying me with a bemused look on his face.

"Yeah," he nodded.

"You saw me time travel?" I asked for confirmation.

His brows rose.

"I'm not quite sure what I saw," he admitted.

I grinned, then hopped back over the line.

"There, did you catch it that time?" I asked teasingly. "I lost and then regained an hour in less than a second. Time travel, baby. That's my superpower!"

He turned his head up to the sky.

"Annie," he said, a smile playing in his voice. "You've made me stop no less than ten times. Two of those times were to pick wildflowers on the side of the road. For the love of God, woman," he turned his face down to me, "can we *please* just get to where we're going? My mom expects us in time for dinner, and I swear to God, if we're late, she'll never let you forget it."

I scrunched my nose at him.

"Okay, but could you just take a pic…"

He got off the bike and started stalking towards me.

I giggled and started to back up.

His brows rose.

"You really want to play this game?" He asked. "I lift, and I run five miles a day. The only time I've ever seen you run was to Chipotle, and the only lifting you do is bringing a burrito to your mouth."

My mouth dropped open in affront.

"You…you… *horrid* man! How dare you!" I yelled, wagging my finger at him.

He grinned, and for the first time, I really saw how happy he was.

But his happiness came from basically calling me fat, and well, there was just no way any woman would ever let that comment go without some sort of reply.

So I did what I had to do—I played dirty.

I turned, then rubbed my eyes so I could get some good tears flowing.

I had been blessed with the ability to cry at will.

It's a good thing, too, because I'd needed that particular skill when it came to dealing with my treacherous sister.

She was the baby in our family, and she got away with almost everything, well, until I started the crying bit.

And my daddy always fell for it—hook, line and sinker.

Mig's arms went around me from behind, and I gave a good fake sob, causing him to freeze.

Then he turned me around so he could see the tears streaming down my face.

"I…I…why are you crying? I didn't mean it, honey," Mig said quickly.

I looked up at him, smiling weakly while I simultaneously reared back to deliver a quick jab to his abs.

He grunted at the hit as he looked down at me in shock.

"What was that for?" He asked, rubbing his belly.

I narrowed my eyes.

"I'll have you know that I have weights in my office that I lift, buddy! And I do yoga. So a Chipotle Burrito isn't the only thing I lift!" I countered smartly.

His lips twitched, and I started shaking my finger at him.

"Don't you dare laugh!" I snapped.

Before I could back up any further, Mig grabbed me just as a truck passed right beside us, making me jump.

I'd been so lost in Mig that I hadn't realized we'd moved closer to the highway.

Jesus.

Mig never missed anything, though, and he saw the truck and got pissed, raising his hand and flipping off the driver who laid on his horn as he passed us.

I wanted to laugh, but I managed not to, instead holding Mig's glare.

Or at least what I assumed was his glare, as he was wearing sunglasses that made it impossible for me to see his eyes.

"So, what happens if I laugh?" He rumbled, dropping his mouth down to nibble on my neck.

I bit my lip as I imagined what I would like to happen.

This little fantasy had him doing all the work.

'I'd make you lick me until your tongue cramps,' was what I wanted to reply. What I said, though, wasn't even remotely similar to what I was thinking.

"You'd be making me breakfast in bed for the next week," I said.

He snorted. "And how would you get me to do that?"

I thought about it and couldn't come up with a logical answer.

Everything that came to mind would have totally defeated the purpose if I had to force him to do it.

His hands started to slide up the back of my shirt, and another horn honked, this one from a big truck.

I jumped, slamming my head into Mig's chin.

Mig growled, then let his hands slip free.

"Alright, it's time to go," he said, taking my hand.

I followed behind him, my hand in his.

He remounted first, grabbing both helmets and waiting for me to take my seat before he handed mine back to me.

"We have another hour or so, then we'll be there," he said.

I secretly thought that was good, because I already had to pee.

Not that I would be telling him that, though.

He'd told me not to drink so much Dr. Pepper, and I really didn't want to hear him say 'I told you so' again.

We exited the highway about ten minutes after we'd gotten back on it, taking a lot of winding roads that felt like they were leading us in circles.

Something I realized later on was the point.

We pulled up to a very formidable looking gate, and Mig punched in some numbers before waiting for it to open.

Once there was enough room, he passed through and started to race up the longest driveway I'd ever seen.

It had to be at least as long as a football field, if not longer.

"This driveway had to have cost a fortune to put in," I said.

Mig nodded his head.

"It did. About fifty grand, if I remember right," he confirmed.

Then we pulled up to an enormous house overlooking the ocean that was probably the same size as my old high school.

It was incredible.

And I was way under-dressed to meet the woman standing on the front porch.

The man was wearing jeans, but they were neatly pressed with a crisp crease down the front of them.

I was not big on ironing, not at all, and I certainly wasn't looking anything other than rumpled after our long trip.

Mig turned the motorcycle off, and I needed a minute for my hearing to clear out the residual echo of his bike.

It took me a moment to notice that Mig was not happy.

His body was practically vibrating with tension.

"What the fuck are you doing here?" Mig asked the man standing in front of him.

"Vitaly, son," he said, his Russian accent thick. "I just had to meet the person responsible for your first call to me in four years."

I blinked.

Mig hadn't spoken to his father in four years? Why?

Mig never spoke badly about his father; in fact, he actually spoke highly of him during the few times he said anything about them at all.

And if I wasn't mistaken, I could've sworn I saw Mig's mother look at Mig's father with not only reproof but also with love.

They've been divorced for years now.

Quite a few years, if I remembered what Mig told me correctly.

But I could definitely see it.

They seemed to naturally gravitate toward each other.

I would bet my last twenty bucks that there was still something between them.

Mig's 'Nonnie' pushed through his parents, who were still standing at the top of the steps, and started towards me.

"Boys," Nonnie said. "How about you do this after we invite our guest inside?"

She was about the size of my mother but much more frail looking.

Her hair, which I'd seen had previously been sheer black in all of Mig's photos scattered around his place, was now a straight sheet of silvery white.

While the two men stayed locked in a silent stare down, Nonnie sighed and grabbed my hand, and led me into the kitchen that was off the side of the living room.

"All that testosterone! Let's give them a few minutes to talk it out," Nonnie's fragile voice said as she shuffled forward.

I followed, very aware it was highly unlikely that either man would back down.

"They aren't gonna start fighting each other, are they?" I asked worriedly.

"No," Mig's mother said from behind me, scaring the crap out of me.

I slapped my hand down on my chest, breathing slightly heavy.

"You scared me," I told her.

She smiled and walked around me to the kitchen counter.

"Would you like something to drink?" She asked, gathering up a basket of what looked like homemade bread and bringing it to the table.

My mouth watered.

I was definitely packing on a few extra pounds while I was here.

"Do you have any sweet tea?" I asked.

She nodded, then went to the fridge while I took a seat where Nonnie shoved me down, her strength surprising for such an old woman.

"Tell me about yourself. Mig's never brought a woman home before," Nonnie ordered.

I smiled, happy at the fact that I was the first woman for the two of them to meet.

So I told them about myself. My job. How Mig and I met. Then I mentioned Jennifer, but quickly caught myself but before I said too much.

"You're kidding," Vada, Mig's mother, said. "And his ex-wife is pregnant? Who is the father?"

She was leaning forward, listening to my every word.

A little too late I realized that maybe I shouldn't have told her Mig's personal business.

But how was I supposed to know that Mig had never told his family about being *married*?

"Yes, she's pregnant. And I already told you Jennifer was coming over here tomorrow," Mig said tiredly as he entered the room, his father, Vitaly Senior, at his back.

"No," Vada said. "What you told me was that you were bringing a woman here that needed protection. Two women that needed protection. One was your woman, and one wasn't."

I wanted to laugh.

That was Mig. King Of Need To Know: he tells you what you need to know and not a single word more.

"So maybe now's not a good time to tell you that you'll be having a grandchild soon?" Mig asked, crossing his arms across his chest.

I could tell just by the way he said it that he didn't mean for it to come out like it sounded.

But the two women in the room started screeching, and suddenly I was surrounded by two very excited women.

"When is the baby due?" Vada asked.

"Oh, you don't look pregnant. I'm so happy for you, Vitaly," Nonnie cooed, gesturing to him.

I was frozen, not knowing what in the world to say to that.

Mig's brows crunched low, as he squeezed his eyes shut.

"Shit," Mig sighed.

Poor guy.

"Mig," I said. "Can you maybe give us a few minutes?"

He looked at me like I'd just saved his life, then gladly took his leave, grabbing his father around the collar as he went.

Vitaly Sr. went willingly enough, but I could tell he was excited to have a grandchild, too.

"Ladies," I said. "I'm not pregnant."

Both stopped cooing and looked at me in confusion.

"But…" Vada started.

I held up a hand.

"Sit down, I need to tell you a story," I said softly.

I could tell by the way the two women sat that they were a little bit disappointed when I'd told them I wasn't pregnant.

And although the thought was a nice one, it wasn't Mig's and my time.

One day, yes. But not now.

Not yet.

"So…there was this girl…"

***

I looked up in sympathy as a physically and emotionally exhausted Mig finally dragged himself through the door of his bedroom.

He'd been talking with his parents and grandmother for a very long time.

I could hear Vitaly Sr. yelling at the top of his lungs—mostly in Russian. I had only been able to make out the basics because all I understood was the word 'Jennifer' from his mouth.

I'd quietly left, closing the door behind me.

Then I'd snuck off to the bedroom I guessed was ours since it was where our bags were.

I'd passed the master, knowing instantly that Mig's father was staying there from the men's socks on the floor.

But there was also women's underwear on the floor.

I didn't go too much further into that room before back pedaling.

I'd also passed Nonnie's room and knew it was hers by all the pictures on the walls from different generations.

The last one I came to must've been solely the guest room since we had our own little entrance and exit to the backyard, although I couldn't see the pool that I knew was there.

I'd been sitting on the bed, looking out over the sprawling lawn, listening to the sounds of the waves crashing into the beach and trying to drown out the yelling.

Now, here I sat with a million questions on my mind.

So I started in on him, even though I knew he needed a break.

But it was time.

I needed to know.

"Mig…why don't you talk to your father?" I asked.

He grimaced, plopping down in a wicker chair that was staged 'just so' against the far wall.

"My father had different ways of making sure I became a 'man', as he liked to call it, and a lot of those ways always ended up with me bleeding," he muttered. "And I resented him for leaving us. I still resent him. He's the reason I stayed with Jennifer as long as I did."

That made sense, sadly.

I hated that he'd had that kind of childhood.

"What do you mean by 'bleeding'?" I asked.

He scrunched up his nose.

It was cute.

Which for Mig, was weird.

"He kicked my ass on a daily basis to make sure I was able to fight in case something ever happened to me, and he couldn't be there to protect me," he said in answer.

I blinked.

"He beat you so you would know how to fight?" I asked in confusion.

He shrugged. "More or less. Put me into martial arts. Jiu Jitsu. Krav Maga. I'm a master in almost everything there is to be a master in, trying to ensure that I had training in a few different techniques."

"So you competed in tournaments?" I asked.

He shook his head, eyes never straying from the ceiling.

"No. Not exactly," he answered cryptically.

"And you did all of that before your military career?" I continued, not giving him a chance to close up.

His mouth snapped shut, and his eyes went blank.

I growled in frustration and stood up, walking towards the door.

"Where are you going?" He asked casually.

I looked at him over my shoulder.

"Away from you and your evasive answers," I snapped as I slammed the door shut and walked out into the dark hallway.

Then even further to the outdoor pool that we'd eaten dinner near earlier that evening.

The pool was one of those infinity pools that overlooked the ocean. I was laying on one of the lounge chairs looking out over the pool to the ocean. Because of how the pool was built parallel to the horizon, the pool looked like it was running right into the ocean.

I was tempted to get in, but I was only wearing a nightgown, having already taken off my bra and panties to get ready for bed… and for Mig.

Not that I'd give him the satisfaction of knowing that right now.

I looked over at the master bedroom, waving slightly when I saw Vitaly flick his fingers in my direction as he locked the French doors, and pulled down the shades.

I turned my gaze back to the pool, the ocean and the horizon, and contemplated my life.

It was in shambles.

I had to contact all of my clients and tell them that I was taking a 'leave of absence' for the foreseeable future. And while I did have a lot saved up (or the insurance money), I wasn't sure my clients would come back after how abruptly I'd shut my salon down. I didn't even get into it with them that it was unsafe, that surely would have been the final nail in the coffin of my little salon.

Which meant that since they didn't know when I'd reopen, they'd have to go to someone else.

Sure, some would come back, but I'd definitely lose even more clients. And I'd already lost quite a few to this situation.

Mig stepped in to my line of sight, and I tilted my head back to pin him with a glare.

"What do you want?" I snapped.

He grinned.

"You."

"Well, you can't have me. I'm going to have to take a pass on your dick for awhile," I told him honestly. "It muddles my thoughts, clouds my brain, and then I starting thinking things are better than they really are."

"Wow," he said, walking around the chair. "I had no idea my dick was that powerful, baby. I mean, yeah he's a big guy and work all kinds of magic, but you make it sound like he's the leader of a cult or something."

I flipped him off, and he laughed as he sat down in between my legs.

His big body forced my legs open wider, and I only let that happen because he would have just sat on them if I didn't.

And I didn't think my legs could handle his bony butt.

He made himself comfortable, turning to face the ocean, as he leaned back against my chest.

When I went to move, he grabbed my flailing arms and wrapped them around his neck.

I wasn't uncomfortable, per se, but I also wasn't comfortable, either, with all of Mig's considerable bulk pressed against me.

"On the back of my neck," he said.

Then he took my hand and moved it until my fingers brushed over a small, puckered scar.

"What's that from?" I asked, no longer wanting to move now that I realized he wanted to talk.

I massaged the spot as he started to talk.

"When I was ten, my dad started my training. That first year he also started entering me into cage fighting matches to test my skills and identify my weaknesses," he said. "I was paired up with kids between five and ten years older than me whose parents also wanted them to learn these same sets of skills."

I blinked.

"Same sets of skills?" I asked carefully.

He nodded.

"Yeah. You wouldn't believe the kind of attention rich kids get. Blackmail, extortion. Not to mention that they're more likely to be targeted for a kidnap and ransom," he said. "Some parents believed, like my dad did, that if they trained their kids to protect themselves, they'd at least be able to fight back if necessary if there ever came a time that they were taken."

"That's...that's insane," I finally decided on.

Mig snorted.

"That was my reality. And every summer and Christmas break, until I was eighteen, was spent training with my father," he sighed. "It was the summer of my fourteenth year that my father decided that maybe I wasn't as good as he had hoped I would be, and he decided to plant a tracking device in my neck during one of the times that I'd been knocked unconscious."

I froze with my thumb covering the scar.

"Is it...is it..." I couldn't finish.

What kind of parent would do that?

Then my gut reaction was just that…to protect.

Vitaly was scared his son would be taken.

So he'd done the unthinkable.

And tagged his son like he was a dog.

"Yeah," he said.

I blinked.

"It is?" I gasped.

He nodded. "Yeah. I found out about it when I went into the Air Force. He came to my boot camp graduation, told me about it when he took me out to dinner…then asked me to leave it in for his peace of mind."

I was silent.

"I went down when I was flying during a training exercise. Fished out of the ocean by a Russian ship, no less," he said. "And held for ransom."

I stayed silent still, waiting for him to continue as my heart started to race.

"They knew my general location, but the Russians were what you would call modern day pirates," he said. "They requested money in exchange for me. And you know the US Government doesn't deal with terrorists."

No, I *didn't* know that.

"My dad found out, even though to this day I don't know how. The Air Force wouldn't have told him anything. They don't usually tell the family unless there's a body, or that I'm alive and recuperating in a hospital."

I didn't know that either.

"I was too banged up to save myself. I had two broken arms, a broken collarbone, and two sprained ankles from the fall into the ocean. I'd deployed my parachute too late; let's just say it's not fun to hit the ocean at the speed I'd been going."

"So your dad saved you?" I guessed.

He nodded.

"And he was disappointed in me," he confirmed.

I blinked.

"For what?" I practically barked.

"For not being able to save myself, I'd guess," he surmised.

I didn't think that was it.

Not at all.

But I would save that conversation for later.

Right now, Mig needed me.

He'd shared some deep stuff with me, stuff I was sure he didn't ever want to share.

"So after I recovered, I got back in, and did some fixing in my life. Got better. Took more chances. Did some things that I never want to do again," he said. "But those things took me to Uncertain, and I'm lucky. I could've been dead with all the things I tried to do," he sighed. "Took stupid risks. Didn't care about the outcome. Until I saw you."

"Me?" I asked.

He nodded. "A year or so after I moved to Uncertain, you were in the parking lot of the diner, talking to a man about buying his car."

I remembered that.

And I remembered exactly the moment he'd come outside.

I hadn't realized he could hear me, though.

"He tried to stiff me," I laughed.

Mig rolled over, doing something at the back of my chair with his hands, and suddenly I was flat on my back.

"Do you know how hot it was to hear you talk to a man about a car, and it was clear you knew exactly what you were talking about?" He asked.

I smiled at the memory.

The guy had thought that, because I was a teenaged girl, I knew nothing about cars.

But I did.

And I'd turned that man down so fast his head had spun.

"I was also the reason you got the car you have today," he said.

I blinked.

I had a nice Cherry Red Mustang.

It ran like a dream, and I'd gotten it for a song.

"Really? How?" I asked.

Then things started to click.

"Was that car yours?" I asked carefully.

He nodded, looking down into my eyes.

"Kind of. I bought it with you in mind. Fixed it up. Then sold it to you by way of Alison's friend," he said.

My mouth gaped.

"You're kidding."

He shook his head.

"No."

And suddenly, I just couldn't help it.

I laughed.

I laughed until I cried.

"You're horrible," I told him.

He grinned, leaned forward even more, and let me feel his erection.

It was then that I realized he only had his underwear on...and I didn't have any.

CHAPTER 23

Please don't be an asshole to Mig. He's had years of experience being an asshole. On the asshole scale, he's an expert, and you're a beginner. There's a big difference between the two.
-Annie's secret thoughts

Annie

I licked my lips, casting a nervous cursory glance around to make sure we were alone.

We were.

The only thing that I could see clearly was the two feet surrounding us.

The soft glow of the moon barely offered enough light to see Mig's face.

But we were outside, and I could tell by the way he was running his lips along the length of my neck that we wouldn't be moving inside.

The nightgown I was wearing was slowly inched up my legs, until it was caught under my ass.

"Lift that pretty, little ass of yours," he whispered gruffly.

I complied, lifting my hips, and subsequently pushing my pussy up against him.

The length of his erection was barely contained by his underwear, and he was hot, hard and oh so ready.

Although, it didn't take much to get him that way lately.

All it took was a stray look on my part, and he was on me.

But I liked it.

I liked it a lot.

My hands ran up his smooth back, coming to a rest on the base of his neck where I worked my hands into what little hair he had.

Dragging my nails against his scalp, I gasped when he bit by shoulder.

My hips jerked, and I could feel the cool cushion of the lounge chair underneath me.

It was rough on my skin, but I barely noticed as Mig finally worked the night gown up and over my head.

As soon as it cleared my chest, his lips latched on to one peaked nipple and pulled.

My hands went up above my head, latching onto the metal of the chair as my body arched to meet him.

He planted one elbow in the cushion next to my head, while the other ran up the length of my body, eliciting goosebumps in its wake.

He was working one breast, and I reached up to palm the other. Mig, seeing this, sucked harder, as a shiver chased up my spine.

"Ticklish?" He asked, doing it again.

This time I wasn't able to withhold the giggle that came with the move, causing him to smile.

"I love you," he said.

My body froze.

"W-what?" I gasped, giving him my full attention.

His mouth went down to run along my collarbone before it descended to my other nipple.

But before he took the peak in his mouth, he growled.

"You heard me."

I *did* hear him.

I just wanted him to repeat it.

Over and over again until the words finally sank in.

He didn't give that to me, though.

Instead, his actions spoke for him—loudly—as he worshipped my body.

The way his hands moved over my body slowly, sensually, communicated his love, devotion and commitment to me.

"One day," he said. "You're going to marry me."

Once again, my body froze, and what little air I was able to get into my lungs froze.

"W-what?"

I sounded like a broken record.

But he was giving me everything I had hoped and dreamed about with him.

Not to mention the way his hands were coasting along on my body, it was no surprise that I couldn't focus in the first place.

He shifted to free his erection from the confines of his boxer briefs.

The sight of his massive frame illuminated by the moonlight, on his knees between my splayed legs, was breathtaking.

Mig was undoubtedly a handsome man, but like this, he was powerfully so.

The moonlight shadowed his face, making the expression of concentration on it look even fiercer.

His abs were rippled and looked even more pronounced than usual.

His erection stood out in front of him: straight, long, thick, and angry.

It was his eyes, though, that I couldn't look away from.

"You got any words for me?" He asked, fisting his cock and working his hand down the length.

I licked my lips, barely containing the urge to bury my fingers inside myself to bring the orgasm that I felt waiting in the wings.

"What words?" I teased.

He started to work his length faster.

His balls swung with the movement, and I started panting.

He'd stay there all night, keeping his hands to himself, if I didn't say the words he knew I felt.

My hands went to my breasts, and I pressed them together to try to ease the ache that I was feeling.

"The love I have for you, Mig, I can't put into words. 'I love you' just doesn't seem to be enough, which was why I haven't said it yet," I told him, pouring my heart out. "I love you more than I've ever loved anyone in my life. And to your other comment, the one about me marrying you, that isn't even a question you need to ask me. I was yours from the moment I saw you ride into town on your black Harley."

He smiled.

Then took a hold of my hips, and roughly turned me over until my stomach was down.

My hips were pulled back, and suddenly I was filled with two fingers.

Two large, rough fingers.

"Always so wet for me. Only me," he growled, pushing his fingers in and out.

But then they were gone just as quickly as they came…but not for long.

Soon I was filled with three.

He pumped them in and out, curling them down to seek out that spot inside of me that always made me shoot off like a bottle rocket.

And just like every other time, I didn't disappoint him.

I came.

Hard.

Clamping down on his fingers like my body never wanted them to leave.

But they did leave.

And when my hips started to sag, he grabbed me with his large hands, and impaled me on his cock.

I stifled a scream in my arm, but only just barely.

He slowly worked his cock into me in short, soft jabs, pulling back and thrusting forward until he was fully imbedded inside of me.

Once he had me completely filled, he started rocking me, not pulling out at all.

It felt amazing, like the two of us were one.

I dropped down until my shoulders met the lounge, and the new angle pushed him impossibly further inside of me.

He growled, and his thrusts became more pronounced.

I gasped when he began to bottom out inside of me.

Normally he was careful with how much he gave me, but when he continued thrusting deeply, I realized that he was out of control.

And that I quite liked the little bit of pain.

His thrusts started to become somewhat frantic, and the loss of his control ignited the loss of mine.

Soon we were both chasing something that neither one of us recognized until much later.

Skin slapped against skin.

Hands grasped for purchase.

Mig pulled my hair.

I dug my nails into his thighs until I drew blood.

And when my orgasm finally slammed into me, I couldn't hold the scream in.

Mig poured himself into me, growling like an animal.

And when the lights turned on in front of us, my brain snapped back into reality.

I squealed and lunged forward, diving for my night gown that was on the floor beside the lounger.

I just barely manage to get it on before the door that I'd seen Mig's father close earlier open again.

I sat down on the lounger, my back to the doors, and stared at Mig's chest.

He was sitting on his ass facing me, thankfully with his penis covered.

But I could tell the second he realized that his parents were sleeping together, because he stiffened slowly.

"Please, for the love of God, tell me that you're not doing what I think you're doing," Mig said to his father.

I covered my face in embarrassment.

It couldn't be much different then what we'd been doing only a few minutes ago!

But I refrained from saying that aloud since I valued my health.

"I could say the same to you, son. Try to keep it down from now on. Next time take it to the lounger in front of your room instead of mine," Vitaly Senior said, shutting the door once he realized all was okay.

My face flamed even more, and I started to laugh.

"Oh, my God," I moaned.

Mig sighed.

"You make me forget myself sometimes," he said softly, pulling my head forward onto his chest.

I wrapped my hands around his waist, resting my cheek against his muscled chest.

"I can't seem to help myself," I teased.

He growled.

"My parents..." he cursed. "They're back together. And let me tell you something, they're horrible together. Fight like cats and dogs. They don't care who's around when they do."

"They love each other," I told him.

He rumbled low in his chest. "Yeah, they do."

I leaned back, letting him see my face.

"Then let them try to find their happy."

He leaned his forehead forward until it leaned against mine.

"Like we found our happy?" He asked softly.

I smiled.

"Yeah, like we found ours."

CHAPTER 24

I'm not telling you it's not going to hurt along the way. What I'm telling you is that it's going to be worth it.
-Mig to Annie

Mig

"I don't see why I can't go with you," I growled.

"Because we have your father here, and the baby needs things. I don't want you around because I'm still upset with you for keeping that viper a secret from us," my mother snapped.

She was pissed.

I knew she would be, which was why I'd put off telling her.

She left without another word, and I looked up at the ceiling, studying the tin roof.

My Nonnie didn't say a word, either.

I could feel her glare, though, as she passed me by.

And swear to Christ, she intentionally stomped my foot with her walker.

"Dad," I stopped him before he could follow my mother out of the house. "Please be careful with her. She's smart, but dangerous situations just seem to find her, and she's got no idea whatsoever about how to protect herself. Please stay close and keep vigilant."

He raised a condescending brow at me.

"I taught you everything you know. Give me a little credit," he said, then slammed the door behind him, leaving me alone in a room with a woman that I absolutely did not want to see.

"Casten," I said.

Casten sighed, giving Annie's dog one last scratch before he stood up and walked out the door, following behind my parents.

I didn't bother looking at Jennifer.

She was upset with me.

And to be honest, I was upset with her, too. It sickened me to have her here, a place that had always been a special place for me.

A place where the outside world seemed so far away.

Jennifer tapped away on her phone, ignoring me as best as she could.

I went onto the back deck and started to make calls, my father helpfully handing me a list of associates he thought might be able to help me with Liam Cornell.

I was lost in a phone call when I felt the first tingle of awareness that something wasn't right.

It was too quiet.

The pool pump, normally a constant hum in the background, wasn't running.

The waterfall, normally a continuous slow trickle, had clearly been off for a while, seeing as the stream was practically dry.

"Shit," I said softly.

"What?" Wolf asked.

"The power's off," I said.

Wolf cursed, and I shoved the phone into my pocket as I slowly stood.

I didn't hang up, though.

With any luck, Wolf would be able to hear all that went on.

And if things went south, he'd be able to get help to Annie if she needed it.

I knew it wouldn't end well for me the moment I turned around and saw Liam standing behind Jennifer.

Jennifer's eyes were filled with sorrow, and I knew she had a hand in this.

Why it never occurred to me that Jennifer would lead the man to my doorstep, I didn't know.

I should have.

In my defense, though, I kept hoping that there was some good in the woman who was carrying my child.

There wasn't.

"Looks like you're alone," Liam said.

I nodded. "I am."

My gun was burning a hole in my back, my hands tingling with the urge to grab it.

But I knew it wouldn't do my any good.

I couldn't get to it fast enough for Liam not to put a bullet through Jennifer, and although she betrayed me, I wouldn't sacrifice her life like that.

However, if I made it out of this alive, and Annie was unhurt, I would see that Jennifer paid for her betrayal.

"You're a hard man to get alone. Always seem to have a man up your ass," Liam said calmly.

I raised my brow at him.

I was alone a lot.

It more sounded like he couldn't get to me when I was alone.

I usually wasn't as stupid as I was being at the moment.

"So, what's your plan?" I asked.

He smiled.

Then turned his gun on me, firing twice.

***

I woke up with my mouth tasting funny.

My tongue stuck to the roof of my mouth like it did when I drank way too much the night before.

But I knew I hadn't done that last night.

Then the feeling of metal surrounding my wrists made me realize that something wasn't right.

My eyes slowly opened, and the sudden, bright light seared my brain.

I groaned as I tried to control the nausea that started to boil in my stomach.

"Ahh, glad to see you're not dead. I shot you with twice as much tranquilizer as I should have because I didn't want to take the chance that you'd wake up before we got here."

The man's snide comments made me force my eyes open again, even though I only wanted to leave them closed and die.

Liam.

Wonderful.

"What do you want?" I slurred.

Liam smiled.

"It's time that I repay you for the mutilation you so kindly provided me," he said, fingering a raised pink scar on his cheek.

I wanted to laugh.

Instead, I looked down, recognizing the bulge of a phone in my pocket, making me realize that the only thing he'd stripped from me was the gun that was at the small of my back in a pancake holster.

Stupid.

Very stupid.

And sloppy.

But I wouldn't need much.

The first explosion of pain only made me more determined.

"So you don't want to do a fair fight? I, at least, allowed you to have your hands free," I spat blood on the floor.

I ran my tongue over my teeth, a little too thankful that the hit didn't knock and of them loose.

I'd managed to make it throughout my whole life keeping my teeth in my head and that was a miracle.

I'd be damned if this man fucked up my streak.

Liam growled.

"Don't you ever stop talking?" He demanded.

I shrugged.

"Yeah, when I'm fuckin' my woman. Then I let my body do the talking," I taunted.

Liam's eyes narrowed.

"That's not what I heard you say in the camera feed I had my boys hack into...quite the dirty mouth you have."

Do not react. Do not react. Do not react.

I repeated that mantra to myself, even when I wanted to break my own fucking hands to get to the fucker in front of me.

"Quite the fat ass you have there," Liam said. "Curves like Annie's aren't in. In fact, I would call her more cow-like than curvy. Even though you tell her she's beautiful. Tell me," he smiled. "What's it feel like to put your cock into somebody that disgusting?"

Do not react. Do not react. Do not react.

I reacted.

I couldn't help it.

I smiled.

And Liam pulled out his brass knuckles.

"Let's see who's laughing in just a few minutes when I make your face unrecognizable for your mother," he said.

This hit hurt exceptionally more.

Partly because he'd hit me with the brass knuckles, and partly because he'd hit me against my temple instead of my jaw.

Stars started to blur my vision, but I still had the smile on my face.

Fucker couldn't take that from me.

I'd keep smiling until it killed me.

"So, tell me," I said during one of Liam's breaks. I was making him winded, and his knuckles were bleeding. Although, some of the blood was mine, but not all. "Why'd you send Jennifer to me?"

Liam pulled a white handkerchief out of his pocket and started to wipe the blood off his hand.

"Before, it was all about you being a DEA agent, and us learning what we could from having someone on the inside. But then we found out you were the baby billionaire of Konn Vodka. We figured out really quick that the quick cash would come from you and what we could get daddy to give us in exchange for not killing you," Liam Cornell snarled. "But now it's all personal. You fucked up doing what you did."

I wanted to laugh.

My father wouldn't pay a damn thing for me.

He trained me since I was old enough to follow directions how to fight.

Vitaly, if you're ever in the situation where you are held for ransom, you show them why it was a stupid idea to do so. You learn how to fight. You practice. You execute. You get out of that situation, because if the time ever comes that you are taken, you won't find me paying them at the other end. Because they won't give you back to me if I pay them. It doesn't work like that.

No, my father wouldn't come.

But my brothers would.

And then I'd be free to get these fuckers off my wrists, and end what I should've finished months ago.

"Why the long look?" Liam asked, shoving the soiled linen into his pants pocket.

I shrugged as best as I could.

"My dad won't be giving you any money. You got nothin' with Jennifer, mostly because she was nothing to me," I said, closing my eyes. "And as for the beating you part, I regret that."

Liam's eyes narrowed.

"Is that right?" He asked smoothly.

I smiled.

He narrowed his eyes.

"That's right. I would've taken you out completely had I known you were going to pull this shit. But I'll remedy that in a little bit when my brothers get here," I explained.

His fists clenched.

"You don't have any brothers," he countered.

"Is that what you think?" I challenged him.

He nodded. "I've had you thoroughly checked out. You have a mother and a father, as well as a grandmother that means very much to you. A girlfriend. A child on the way. But no brothers."

I closed my eyes once again and tried to blank out the pain.

It didn't work, especially when Liam pushed me over, chair and all.

My hands were tied behind my back, so when he pushed me backward, all of my upper body weight landed on my arms and hands.

It felt delightful.

Not.

My right shoulder screamed, and I knew instantly it was out of socket.

That'd be a bitch to get put back.

My left hand also felt slightly off, which probably meant it was broken, thanks to the metal cuffs and the awkward tilt to my hand where it'd been secured.

On the bright side, however, the wooden slats on the chair broke, freeing my arms.

And although it'd hurt like a motherfucker, I'd be able to get my hands in front of me since my shoulder was dislocated.

Which was going to happen earlier than I thought it would seeing as Liam's phone rang.

He left without doing anything else to me, and I waited about twenty seconds after the door closed, then rolled.

The pieces of wood from the broken chair rolled free, and I stood up on a wave of pain.

Vision blurring, I slowly worked my hands under me, one leg at a time, until they were no longer behind me.

Bile rising in my throat, I walked determinedly to the far wall where there was a pillar for support.

Then, gritting my teeth, I roughly slammed my arm into the wall.

It didn't pop in until the third attempt, and a blast of pain roared through me at the accomplishment.

My knees started to buckle, but the door to the side of me started to open, and it took every bit of strength I had left to launch myself.

Unfortunately, it was one of the good guys, and Liam.

Lucky for me, Casten decided not to completely annihilate me.

He only threw me over his shoulder, or tried to.

The cuffs around his neck held strong, and although I was seconds away from vomiting, I managed to let go before I did any more damage to myself or Casten.

"Motherfucker," Casten growled. "Why'd you have to go and do that?"

He was rubbing his neck, and I wanted to laugh.

However, I knew if I laughed, I'd be in too much pain afterward to make my body move.

"You take care of him?" I asked, sitting as still as I possibly could.

"Negative," he said, closing the door.

He helped me to my feet, then surveyed my face.

"You look good," he lied.

I winked at him.

"I'm trying some new makeup," I grunted as I got my feet firmly on the ground beneath me. "Got a gun?"

He pulled a handcuff key out of his pocket, quickly removed the cuffs, and then shoved my own Glock into my hand.

The familiar weight of it felt heavenly.

"Annie?" I asked.

"Fine. Got a call from Wolf, then followed your signal here," Casten said, answering my next question before I'd even asked it.

I nodded.

"Wolf still on the line?" I asked, checking the gun's chamber.

Still loaded with my hollow points.

Good.

"Yeah, listened the entire time you got your face rearranged," Casten replied almost soundlessly.

He went to the door, listened, and then opened it with nary a sound.

He pulled out a compact that looked vaguely familiar, but I couldn't make my brain work long enough to figure out exactly where it'd come from.

I probably had a concussion…among other things.

"Clear," Casten said.

I followed him, keeping my back to him as I cradled the gun in my good hand, but bad arm.

The shot wouldn't be pretty, and it'd hurt like a mother, but it'd get done if I had to take anyone out.

Something I had to do a few moments later when we got into a boat house, of all places.

It was a young man, one I remembered seeing on a flyer that'd crossed my office desk.

He'd been wanted for suspicion of selling drugs.

And the moment I saw him round the corner into the room we were standing in, I shot him in the leg.

I'd been aiming for the torso.

"Shit," Casten said, rushing faster to the fallen man.

He removed the gun from the man's back, did a quick tap down, and produced a set of keys.

Boat keys, to be specific.

"Bingo," Casten said, standing up.

Then he took him out of the equation with a swift kick to the head that knocked him right the fuck out.

"Should've finished him," I muttered, keeping an eye out.

Casten didn't say anything.

I didn't either.

We walked to the boat, Casten's hands filled with two guns now, instead of just one.

"Gotta open the door and push off," I said, gesturing for him to get into the boat.

He didn't argue.

Instead, he got in, started the large boat up and waited for me to untie us.

It was a good thing, too.

Because, otherwise, I wouldn't have seen the fucking trap door.

Catching Casten's eyes, I gestured to the door, and then slipped through.

It was open, and I assumed that this was where the man Casten had taken down had been coming from when he rounded the corner and saw us.

I got down on my knees, leaning down to get a better look inside the opening, being sure not to put any weight on my bad arm.

And what I saw made my jaw drop.

"Holy Fuck."

I looked up in time to see Casten take out the guy out that'd tried to sneak up on my blind side.

"Fuck," I said, quickly untying the boat.

Then I reached inside the trap door, grabbed a brick of marijuana, and tossed it up and over the bow of the boat.

Casten caught it, and I went to the garage door opener and hit the switch.

I should've known this had been too easy.

The next few minutes played out like a re-enactment of what happened at the OK Corral.

Gun fire was exchanged.

Bodies hit the ground.

The water.

Boats.

Luckily, Casten and I were good at what we did.

Hitting a moving target was a skill we'd both mastered.

These boys, however, probably had never shot at a moving target in their lives.

And it showed as they missed us, repeatedly.

Surprisingly, the only half way decent shot was Liam.

He hit above my head not once, but twice.

I dropped down to my belly and slipped into the water that was rolling with waves from all the boat traffic in the bay.

The salt in the water burned my injuries, and I was rethinking the wisdom of my decision to get in the water.

The hull of the boat protected me as I moved around the front of the boat, then down the other side.

Liam was still aiming at the spot where I'd been, which was his fatal mistake.

I aimed, then fired.

The difference between me and Liam…I didn't miss.

Lani Lynn Vale

CHAPTER 25

Vodka mixes well with everything except decisions. Drink
responsibly.
-Konn Vodka T-shirt

Mig

"Oh, God. You look terrible," she whispered.

I looked up from where I was hunched over in the hospital bed.

It was the only position I could find that didn't make my body ache so
badly that I wanted to barf.

Despite the fact that the nurse had been kind enough to provide me with
not just a painkiller, but an anti-nausea medicine.

I smiled slightly, hating the way her face broke out in despair when the
movement split my lip open once again.

"Thanks," I muttered dryly.

She placed her hands on my chest.

"Is there anything I can get you?" She whispered brokenly.

I nodded, wincing once again when the movement made pain explode in
my brain.

"Yeah," my voice cracked. "Come 'ere and give me a kiss."

Annie came, pressing her lips whisper soft against mine.

I appreciated the effort on her part, but right then I needed more than just a peck.

I needed to feel alive, to prove to myself that I didn't die in that hell hole due to my own stupidity.

I deepened the kiss, and although I tasted blood, I kept pushing the kiss until we both had to stop due to shortness of breath.

"Enough of that now, boy," Nonnie called, entering the room at her usual snail's pace. "Thought for sure I'd have to walk back out because the clothes were gonna come off," she huffed and sat down in the chair next to the bed. "And I barely got here as it is. Not to mention if I fell, my Life Alert button wouldn't produce any hot firemen. Instead, I'd get ugly nurses who do nothing for me."

I laughed.

I couldn't help it.

My Nonnie never ceased to amaze me.

"Do you want me to get you something to drink, Nonnie?" Annie asked, worry evident in her voice.

"No. I have something to drink right here," Nonnie said, pulling out a bottle of vodka. "Want some?"

Konn Vodka, to be specific.

"Uh, no. It's three in the morning, and I don't usually imbibe so late. It makes me restless," Annie said, sounding like she wanted to laugh.

Nonnie twisted off the lid and looked at me pointedly.

"That woman is in labor," Nonnie said, sounding as if she could care less about the situation.

Really it was because 'that woman' had nearly gotten her grandson killed.

I'd known Jennifer was in labor, too.

She was under protective custody until she had the baby. Then, once she was healed enough to be released, she'd be arrested and charged with all the crimes she'd committed.

From what I'd learned from Casten, only minutes before, Jennifer hadn't really wanted to get me killed.

Apparently, she was more scared of Liam than she'd been of me and had done the only thing she thought she could do.

Tell Liam where I was.

What it had done, though, was snowballed and slammed her right in the face.

Now she was looking at accessory to attempted murder, conspiracy to the kidnapping of a federal officer, along with the date rape charges.

I couldn't get her out of those if I tried.

But, I wouldn't even try.

After all I'd done for Jennifer—despite what she'd done to me—she still didn't hesitate to sacrifice me.

"I know. What floor is the maternity ward on?" I asked.

"The fourth. I've already been up there to check on her," Annie said.

"I wanted to say she wasn't in labor, but Casten said her water broke when the police officers placed her under arrest," I observed.

Annie nodded.

"We got home to an empty house, and Jennifer sitting on the couch eating popcorn," Annie said softly. "It didn't look different at all. No sign of a struggle, nothing out of place. But we knew something was up when Casten talked to your father."

I nodded, waiting for her to continue.

"Your father brought us home immediately, walked into the house and started yelling at Jennifer," Annie said.

"I would've snatched the witch up by her hair," Nonnie offered her input.

I snorted.

Annie laughed.

"I was on the verge of doing that too when the police officers got there," Annie supplied. "Would've done it, too, but they took her into custody so fast that I thought she was going to get whiplash."

I sighed.

"She's so fuckin' screwed," I told them. "I've done all I can, but she's still going to serve ten years, *minimum*."

Annie snorted. "I hope the bitch serves life. Or possibly dies in there."

Nonnie made agreeing sounds, and I smiled.

"So how much longer until the baby gets here?" I asked her.

Annie shook her head.

"She kept screaming at me and throwing so much of a fit that I had to leave before she hurt herself or others," Annie explained.

I growled in frustration, then threw the blankets off of me.

"Go get a nurse to take this out for me, please. I'm going to get dressed, then I guess I'll go up there and see her."

My voice sounded as tired as I felt.

And Annie must've realized it, because she didn't argue at all.

"Okay," she whispered. "Don't move too fast."

I gave her a salute and got out of the bed, careful of the IV that was in my forearm.

They'd been pumping me full of fluids through the line, and I had to pee worse than I'd ever had to pee before.

I moved like an old man as I shuffled my feet forward, one after the other, to the bathroom.

"I can see your butt," Nonnie called from behind me.

I held up a thumb.

Nonnie laughed.

"It's the only thing that doesn't have any bruises. Annie should be happy."

I shut the door on her laughter.

"Look, you're on the news!" Annie yelled through the door. "Your ass looks awesome in those jeans. You can't even tell you're hurt!"

I turned my eyes to the wall and just shook my head.

I hadn't realized it until about thirty seconds after waking up from my pain med-induced haze, but I was scared.

Scared that I wouldn't be who I needed to be for Annie and my child.

But all she had to do was yell about how good my ass looked and all of my worries seemed to slip away.

Sort of.

With a baby on the way, there were about fifteen thousand more worries that were about to be placed on my plate.

And I was scared shitless.

***

"Get her out of here," Jennifer hissed.

I wanted to laugh.

"No," I said.

She narrowed her eyes. "I'm not complaining that you're keeping my kid. I'm not complaining that I'll be leaving the only home I know. What I am asking you is that you give me this, and the first hour, and I'll be gone."

I wanted to argue.

But I also felt that maybe she did deserve it, not because she was a good person, but because she was having her child taken away from her, and she'd be spending at least the next ten years in prison.

"I'll wait outside," Annie whispered.

I watched her leave, wondering if I should follow her.

"Alright, ladies and gentlemen. Let's have a baby," the doctor called.

I nodded.

I was surprisingly nervous.

I didn't wish any ill will upon Jennifer.

It made my stomach hurt that she had to go through a surgery to have my child because she could die if she didn't.

And I'd lied earlier.

I was sympathetic to her situation.

I don't know what I would've done to kick the habit of drugs. I know she went through the whole rehab thing when she first got pregnant, paying for it with the money she got from drugging and raping me.

I've never been in that type of situation.

But I do know that I wouldn't have gone about it the same way she did.

I wouldn't have put my body on the line for drugs. I wouldn't trade my life for another's.

And I wouldn't have brought an innocent child into this world all because of a lie.

So I would give her the surgery by herself.

But that would be it, and then she'd be gone.

And it would be Annie, me and the baby.

Annie would be the one that my child thought of as his or her mother.

Annie would be the one the baby went to when it needed something.

I'd be there, too, of course, but the point I was trying to make was that Annie would be everything that Jennifer should have been.

Things moved quickly after that.

I'd arrived at the room in time to overhear the nurse and the doctor speaking with Jennifer about the baby's heartbeat and how it would drop with every contraction.

I'd been the one to tell Jennifer that she needed to go ahead with the surgery seeing as she was extremely adamant about not having a caesarean section.

Once she'd agreed, the nurse and the doctor left the room to get ready for the emergency surgery, leaving me alone with Jennifer for the first time without anyone else in the room to overhear what I was about to tell her.

"You fucked up today," I told her. "I had a way out for you. You had your entire life before you, a fresh start, and now you have nothing."

Jennifer hung her head.

"I know. I didn't have a choice, though. He'd have killed the baby," Jennifer said.

"And how do you know that? Maybe if you'd given me the chance to fix this, you wouldn't be spending the next ten years in an eight by eight cell," I said, crossing my arms stiffly over my chest.

Everything hurt, and I quickly realized that there would be no crossing my arms in the future, possibly for the next couple of weeks.

I had a fractured wrist that was in a bright green cast.

A sore shoulder from my dislocation.

Multiple lacerations on my face from the brass knuckles and Liam's fists.

But at least I was alive.

And I would recover.

Jennifer hadn't known I would get out of it alive, though.

She'd been looking out for herself, even if she had said it was all for the baby.

Another contraction hit Jennifer, and I watched in terror as the baby's heart rate went from 143 to 89.

The nurses rushed into the room then.

One handed me a pair of scrubs, foot booties, and a mask.

"Get dressed. I'll wait here until you're done, then I'll take you back to the OR," the nurse instructed.

I nodded, going into the bathroom and taking off the pair of jeans Annie had brought me, and slipping my legs into the scrubs that were on the verge of being too short.

The scrub top didn't fit very well, but I didn't really care seeing as my shoulder felt like it was on the verge of falling off.

I grunted, maneuvering my arm into the scrub top, but I had to hand the mask to the nurse once I got back outside.

"I can't get this on. It hurts to lift my arm above my bottom rib," I told her.

She slipped the mask on, tying the two ends so the mask laid against my face just so.

Then she gestured for me to follow.

I did and was bombarded by Annie taking pictures of me the entire time I walked down the hall.

"What are you doing?" I asked her, liking the way she was smiling so big.

"I'm documenting this day," she said happily. "The next time I see you, you'll be a daddy."

I grinned at her, even though she couldn't see it.

"Thanks," I said. "Wait here for me, okay?"

I gestured to the corner of the wall right outside of the operating room, and followed the nurse in.

It was freezing.

And Jennifer was already strapped down to a table with both of her arms held out wide beside her.

She had on a blue cap similar to mine, and her eyes were closed.

"She's been knocked out," the nurse said when she caught my wariness. "We don't have time to put in a spinal block or epidural. Just sit down right there, and we'll get the baby to you as soon as we can."

They'd all been prepared, and knew the situation.

Plus, it wasn't their first rodeo.

There was a prison located about fifteen miles from the hospital, and from what I'd learned after I'd told them what was going on, they had women from the prison coming in all the time to have their babies.

They knew protocols and would hand the baby over to me as soon as he or she was checked over.

I was nervous.

Would I be a good father?

Would all of this work out with Annie?

Would she marry me?

Would she be any better at taking care of a child than I would?

All of these thoughts swirled through my brain as the minutes passed by.

Then suddenly, my world stopped.

The sounds of my child's cries filled the room, loud and pissed way the fuck off.

"Oh, he's upset," the doctor drawled.

He.

I had a boy.

I had a boy!

I looked up in time to see the doctor pass my son off to a waiting nurse who had her hands outstretched with a blanket covering them.

She curled her arms around him expertly, and brought my son over.

Then she handed him to me.

"What do you think?" She asked.

I looked at my son.

At the child that was conceived not in love, but during a desperate circumstance, and I couldn't love him any more.

I'd been indifferent about the entire situation since I'd found out about it.

Thought about giving him up for adoption.

Thought about having Jennifer abort the baby.

But now that he was in my arms, I couldn't imagine ever not having him.

He was mine.

And he was perfect.

He had a red splotchy face, a set of lungs that I could just tell would be fun in the future, and a head full of hair that looked exactly like mine.

He had my nose. My hair line.

My everything.

He looked nothing like Jennifer, and for that, I was thankful.

Because I didn't want to look at my son and be reminded of the fact that he was conceived in such an awful way.

I wanted to look at him and be proud, just as I was now, with what I had.

And Vitaly did make me proud.

Vitaly Andrew Konn.

CHAPTER 26

I didn't mean to gain this much weight. It happened by
snackcident.
-Annie's secret thoughts

Annie

I was supremely nervous.

I put on a good show, but I was a mass of nerves as I waited for Mig to come back out of the operating room with his child.

Would it be a girl or a boy?

I'd asked Mig why he didn't know a few weeks ago, and he'd said that he didn't want to know, because it didn't matter.

As long as he or she was healthy, he'd be happy.

And I found that I quite liked the way he thought.

"You need to give them some time before you go in there," a nurse said callously at my side.

I blinked, turning to her.

It was the one who'd walked Mig into the room.

How she'd gotten out when she'd entered was beyond me, but I wouldn't be investigating.

"I'm giving them their time," I said, somewhat annoyed that she even had the gumption to say something like that to me.

She didn't know my story. She didn't know Mig. Nor did she know what Jennifer had done to Mig.

All she knew was that I was the other woman, and had decided to judge.

I decided the best choice would be to not respond.

Instead I stood there, waiting for the doors to the operating room to open.

"You're ignoring me," the nurse said.

She was right. I was.

"I don't know what gave you that idea," I replied softly, my heart beating quickly in my chest.

Was that a cry?

It sounded like a cry!

Then the doors to the operating room opened, and out came a very happy Mig, a smile about a mile wide on his face.

I started taking pictures.

This was too good not to document forever.

I'm so glad that I brought my camera!

"Oh," I breathed when Mig stopped in front of me.

I went up on my tippy toes, then peeked over the side of the blanket.

"It's a boy," Mig rumbled, pride evident in his voice.

My eyes went up to meet his, and a smile transformed my face.

"Congratulations," I said softly.

He winked.

"Want to hold him?" He asked.

I did. I *so* did.

I took about fifteen more pictures, then squirted my hands with the hand sanitizer that was on every corner in the hospital.

Once I'd lathered up my hands, I nervously held them out.

Mig placed his baby into my arms, and I started to cry.

Not pretty tears, either.

"Oh, Mig. You did so good," I whispered.

I looked up at him.

He was looking at me, looking at his son.

"I thought I would hate him," he started.

I knew that, too.

I knew that was why he hadn't bought any clothes.

I knew that was why he really refused to know what the sex of the baby was.

I knew that was why I'd never heard him talk about his excitement at having a baby.

Because this baby was made, not out of love or passion, but desperation. Hate.

Jennifer had done that to him.

Had hurt him.

And Mig hadn't been able to let that go. Hadn't been able to celebrate like most expectant fathers do.

And he'd been in pain.

So much pain that I could see it on his face now.

"Mig," I started.

He started to reply, but shook his head when he saw someone come out after him.

"I've got the extra band if you'd like to have it," a new nurse said, offering it to Mig.

"Can you put it on my fiancé?" He asked.

The nurse jolted, and I could hear the other nurse's scoff at my side.

I didn't bother looking at her.

"Yes, I can do that," she confirmed.

So that was how I'd been given the hospital bracelet that the mothers wore indicating that the baby was theirs.

Mig had an identical one on his wrist, albeit much larger.

"Well, if y'all want to follow me to the nursery, we'll get baby Vitaly cleaned up for you, and then we'll give you a room of your own," the nurse said, sounding jovial.

I would love this job.

Who wouldn't want to help deliver life every day?

"Do you...do you think," Mig said once he got to the door. "Do you think you could go in there with him? I need to go sit with Jennifer while she wakes up. Explain what's going to happen now. But I don't want him to be alone."

My heart hurt.

Jennifer may have been a bad person, but I knew that this had to be hard on her.

"Yeah, I can do that. I'll go in there with him," I whispered. "Then we'll wait for you in the room they give us. Do you think you can wait long enough to tell your Nonnie which room?"

"It'll be the same one we had the mother in earlier," the nurse at my side said. "We'll move Ms. Konn to another room."

I nodded.

"Thank you," I said.

Mig wrapped his arms around both me and his son, pressed his lips against my forehead, then left.

"I hope you got your camera ready," the nurse said. "Because you're about to get some good pictures of us cleaning him up and giving him his first bath."

I was nervous.

I looked down at the little boy that looked so much like Mig that it hurt, and I smiled.

"Yeah, I've got my camera ready," I confirmed.

And boy did Mig's boy scream.

Vitaly Andrew Konn was going to be a bruiser, too.

He was eight pounds and twenty inches long, a healthy weight for a full term baby.

"His lungs sound great, don't they?" The nurse asked.

I nodded.

"Yeah, they do," I confirmed, snapping another picture.

I looked up when someone tapped on the glass, then grinned and waved.

All of the members of the Uncertain Saints were outside, looking through the glass at me and Vitaly.

Peek, Wolf, Ridley, Core, Casten, and Griffin.

Then there was Alison holding Wolf's son, Nathan, squeezed in under Peek's arm.

She gave me wide eyes, and I held up my fingers, signaling he was eight pounds.

"Looks like you've got an excited bunch out there," the nurse observed.

I smiled and studied Mig's brothers.

They were excited, even though they'd never admit it.

They were all badasses...it was badass rule number one: do not show any emotion other than badass.

And, apparently, being excited about a tiny little baby wasn't allowed...not that they were hiding it well.

"Yeah, they're pretty excited," I agreed.

"Here, I'll let you do this," she said, handing me the diaper.

I looked at it, then looked at Vitaly.

He was still screaming, and even though the room was warm, he most certainly was not happy about being out in the open where he could flail his arms.

"Okay," I took the diaper, then opened it.

Then I studied Vitaly to see how best to pick him up and get his underneath of him.

"Here," she said, placing it down on the table.

Then she lifted his legs, which pulled his little booty in the air, and placed him back down on top of the diaper.

"Now do it," she ordered.

I did as she instructed, and I had to admit, I was quite proud of myself.

"It'll get easier the more you do it," she laughed. "Now I'll teach you the art of swaddling."

And damned if she didn't swaddle Vitaly up like a little baby burrito.

She even did it better than Chipotle.

"Wow," I said. "You're good at that."

She winked, then placed Vitaly into my arms.

His eight pounds felt like a solid, secure weight in my arms, and I wanted to hold him forever and ever.

Mig might protest that, though.

So I'd be nice and give him a turn…every once in a while…when I felt like it.

"Alrighty," she said. "I've got your foot and hand prints. We can take him back to your room now, and I'll bring you a bottle in just a few minutes so you can feed him."

"Okay," I said hesitantly.

She caught my hesitance and laughed.

I walked slowly out of the room, smiling widely when I was bombarded by men at least a foot taller than me.

"Let me hold him," Peek demanded.

"No. He's mine," I glared at him.

Then skirted past him, walking into the room.

Sadly, I did end up giving him up to not only the Saints, but also Mig's mother, father and Nonnie, as well.

I'd just gotten him back into my arms with a bottle in his mouth when Mig walked in.

He looked haggard.

Terrible, in fact.

His photos of this day would forever be a bittersweet reminder of Mig's immense joy as well as his pain.

But the minute he saw me holding Vitaly, feeding him a bottle, his face split into a smile.

"You want him?" I asked when he made it up to my side.

I was sitting on the bed, reclining as I fed the baby.

He'd already scarfed down about a half an ounce.

"No," he said. "My arms about to fall off, and I'm scared if I try to hold him, I'll hurt either him or me."

I scooted over, only then realizing that he was dead on his feet.

"Lay down," I ordered him.

He didn't argue, which only went to show just how poorly he was feeling.

He laid down next to me, completely ignoring the others in the room, and leaned his head against mine.

Then he fell asleep, his hand on my leg, just underneath where Vitaly was resting against me.

And he slept.

The others spoke around us, but I was lost in this new world.

A world where Vitaly Andrew the Third and Vitaly Junior were my sole focus.

CHAPTER 27

Shh, there's wine in here.
-Coffee Cup

Annie

Hours later, I was still in the little world Mig had created for me.

I'd just gotten up, leaving Vitaly to Mig, and stretched my legs.

Plus, I had to pee.

Mig had practically fallen asleep on top of me, and he'd not moved for a very long time.

People had slowly trickled out, and now we were left with only Nonnie, and his parents.

They were all discussing what they were wanting for dinner, so I took the chance to get up and leave.

I needed a few moments.

My chest felt so full right now that I needed somewhere to just let it out.

And I found it in the bathroom stall at the very end of the corridor, near the waiting room.

And I cried.

I cried hard.

I didn't know why.

Well I did, and I didn't.

Mostly, it was because today was eventful.

Today had been terrible...and oh so beautiful.

I'd nearly lost Mig, and I never even had him completely to myself.

I wanted him.

I wanted his son.

I wanted to be a mother and a wife.

And I couldn't say that, because Mig was going through enough as it was.

He didn't need me adding to that.

I was in limbo.

I would be until I got this off my chest.

But I wouldn't say a word about it until I got home. Until Vitaly was a few weeks old. Maybe even more.

I was crying so hard, in fact, that I didn't even realize I wasn't alone anymore until two huge, strong arms went around my middle.

I'd been sitting on the toilet, fully dressed.

I'd gone into a stall, and had ensconced myself inside, thinking surely Mig would never follow me here.

I was wrong.

"Why are you crying?" He asked gruffly.

I couldn't tell him that.

But I could tell him that he'd scared me today, which I did.

Loudly.

"You scared me," I sobbed. "I almost lost you."

Mig groaned and took a seat on his ass, leaning his back against the tiled wall.

It was gross to sit on the bathroom floor, but I didn't tell him that.

He had a weird look on his face.

"I was convinced I was going to die today," he admitted.

I looked up at him, tears streaming down my face.

"Don't say that."

I needed him to tell me he knew he'd be ok…not agree with me.

"I did. And it was all because of some woman who used me. Got herself pregnant against my will. Then got me to marry her," he said, leaning his head against the tile and looking up at me.

I didn't say anything.

What was there to say?

What Jennifer had done was awful.

Beyond awful.

But could I say anything against her when she produced something as lovely as Vitaly?

Yes, I could.

But Vitaly was a light at the end of the tunnel.

He was proof that if God brought you to it, God would bring you through it.

"And as I was telling her that she'd never see her son again, besides the picture you sent me," he rasped. "I felt bad…for her. At what *I'd* done to *her*."

I didn't say anything to that.

"And as I was leaving, I realized just how much I love you," he said. "When I got to the room and saw you feeding my son, I realized that I'd never be able to live without you again. The thought of you not there when I wake up physically hurts."

"That's your bruised ribs," I teased.

My tears were slowing, but they were still there.

However, I was always ready for a good joke.

And I'd do anything to get that look off Mig's face.

Defeated.

"I want to ask you to marry me…but I don't want you to think it's only because of the baby," he said, making my heart start to pound.

I waited.

And it was good I did, because he wasn't finished.

"But then I'm a selfish fucker, and I couldn't wait. I needed you to know that I love you, and that I want to spend the rest of my life with you. So I followed you out here, and broke in when I heard you crying in the bathroom," he said, finally turning his eyes to me.

They were bruised.

Huge purple and blue bruises lined his face.

His lip was still split.

His nose was slightly crooked.

And he was the most handsome man in the entire world.

"I love you, too," I said quietly.

He smiled.

"That's why I want you to marry me. You're gonna say yes. And we're going to build a new house, way the fuck away from any of our old memories," he said. "We're gonna make new ones. We're gonna live our life. And we're going to be fuckin' happy."

I wanted to laugh.

He deemed it, so it would be true.

"Oh, yeah?" I asked, dropping down to my knees at his side.

He nodded.

Simple. Easy as that.

"And what makes you think I'll say yes?" I teased, running my thumb over his lip so slightly that it barely even registered as a touch.

"You'll say yes."

My brows rose.

"And how do you know that?" I persisted.

He grinned.

Even though I could tell it was painful, he did it anyway.

Hooking me around the waist, he stood up, then walked out to the bathroom counter and set me on top of it.

I blinked, surprised at the sudden movement.

Then he walked to the door and flipped the lock.

"What are you doing?" I asked, starting to get down.

He was there in the next instant, stilling my movement with a hand on my belly.

"Stay," he ordered, pushing up the skirt I was wearing in ungodly slow movements.

I bit my lip.

"You're hurt," I tried.

He shook his head.

"I'm not too hurt to prove to you just why you want to marry me," he informed me, yanking my hips to the very edge of the counter.

I gasped when I was suddenly up against his hard erection.

Very hard.

Then my panties were shoved to the side, and I was being filled up with Mig's hard cock.

I groaned.

"We need to get you some more slip on pants," I panted.

He didn't reply, but I could tell he liked the thought of easy access for me by the way he started to thrust.

Frantic.

All consuming.

I watched him as he watched me.

His eyes stayed on mine even when mine started to go hooded.

His balls smacked against my ass at the frantic movements.

His breathing was rough.

Mine was even more so.

His hard, thick cock plowed into me.

He was out of control, but then again, so was I.

We were having sex in a public bathroom.

He was hurt.

I was desperate.

And the entire moment was fucking beautiful.

We went over the edge together.

His come filling me up, and his love repairing my nearly shattered heart.

"So is that a yes?" He asked.

I smiled against his neck.

"Yeah, that's a yes," I told him.

He rumbled in happiness, then leaned back and reached into his pocket, only wincing slightly when his bad shoulder started to make itself known again.

And he produced a ring, a simple silver band.

"I was going to get you a big diamond," he said. "But I wanted you to be able to wear it when you were cutting hair or massaging your clients."

I looked into his eyes as he slipped the ring over my finger.

And when it was finally in place, I leaned my head forward, placing my lips against his heart.

"I think you've just made me the happiest woman in the world," I informed him.

He grunted.

"I know."

Lani Lynn Vale

EPILOGUE

My sister said I treat her like a child, so I gave her a sticker for standing up for herself.
-Text from Annie To Mig

Mig

Two weeks later

"If you ever...*ever* tell anyone I took lessons for this dance, I will kick your ass and make sure your face matches your arm," I growled at Casten.

Casten grinned unrepentantly.

"I don't think I'll ever be able to do this justice, though," Casten jeered.

I narrowed my eyes, but decided to let it go.

"Just make sure you get the stupid fucking music up so I can get this shit done," I growled, tugging my shirt at the back of my neck and pulling it over my head.

I threw the shirt on the floor next to the pile of clothes I was to wear, glaring at the stupid monkey suit I was supposed to be wearing.

"I can't wear this," I muttered to myself.

Then I smiled.

I'd wear it...but only the pieces I chose.

***

The moment my eyes lit on Annie as she exited the little cottage at the front of the lawn, my lungs froze in my chest.

My God, she looked beautiful.

So fuckin' beautiful my heart hurt.

The feeling in my chest started to spread and soon nothing else existed but her.

God, she was something.

Her frown didn't even make me wary.

The beautiful smile she gave me when she got mid-way to me and could see my complete outfit made me happy, though.

She knew me.

And she didn't care that I only wore half of what she'd asked me to.

I had the white button down shirt. The dress shoes. But my jeans and cut finished the ensemble.

It was me, and I liked that she liked it.

But she frowned when she was two rows away from me and started to look around in confusion.

Then her eyes lit on Vitaly, my son—our son—and she smiled.

She patted her father on the arm to get his attention, then broke off from her father's hold and walked to Nonnie who was holding Vitaly securely in her arms.

Nonnie gave Annie a glare when Annie gestured for the baby, but nonetheless handed him over.

I smiled widely as she snuggled Vitaly into her arms, propping him up on her chest, then walked back to her father.

I smiled even further when, once she got to me and I took her hand from her father, she handed Vitaly to me.

I loved my son.

He was my perfect mini-me.

And I loved that Annie loved Vitaly like he was her own.

I knew that he'd never feel unloved, because Vitaly was still just as much a part of Annie even if he wasn't of her flesh. She loved him with her whole heart, and I would forever be grateful.

Annie had dressed Vitaly in the smallest little tux I'd ever seen.

Hell, I didn't even realize they were made that small.

But, somehow, Annie was able to pull it off in the two week time limit I'd given her for our wedding.

Her mom, sister, and my mom had accomplished a lot, in fact.

And done a damn fine job of it.

"You ready?" The minister asked.

Annie smiled.

"Almost," she said, hurrying back to Nonnie.

There, she grabbed the burp rag that my son had started requiring since he'd started eating more, and placed it over my shoulder.

I rolled my eyes and repositioned Vitaly in my arms.

We'd found that the best way to situate him was up so he didn't lose his previous bottle.

See, he had acid reflux, and it enabled him to projectile vomit about six feet in front of him.

So we tried to circumvent it before it happened.

And what better way to commemorate the wedding than to have him vomit like that, and every single camera in the room catching it.

Thankfully, I didn't have anyone behind me, because that's what he did in the next moment.

Swear to Christ, it never ceased to amaze me at how well he could aim it.

"Shit," Annie said, watching in horror as Vitaly finally laid his head back down once he was done, almost like a sleepy little drunk who didn't have a care in the world.

The crowd was stunned silent, and I couldn't help the small laugh that leaked out of me at their amazement.

"See, I told you!" I pointed at Casten.

Casten held his hands up. "I was wrong. You were right. It is impressive."

"I hope you got that on camera," my father said, I guessed, to the camera chick who Annie had hired to take photos of us, since I didn't bother to turn around.

I wasn't mad at him anymore.

I knew he was just doing what he thought was best. However, I would never be raising Vitaly like that.

He would know what love was, and I would prove it to him by showing his mother every day that I was graced to have her.

"If you'll both turn to face each other, we'll start the vows," the priest said.

When I faced Annie once again, I studied her.

She had her heart in her eyes, as she always did.

And she looked so beautiful.

"You look beautiful," I said, interrupting the priest.

Annie smiled.

"Thank you," she mouthed.

"Annie, do you take Vitaly to be your husband, to have and to hold from this day forward?"

"I do," she responded firmly.

I wanted to laugh at how sure she sounded.

"And do you, Vitaly…"

"I do."

The crowd laughed.

But I didn't need him to say that stuff.

I knew it like I knew I'd draw my next breath.

I'd give anything and everything to have Annie forever at my side.

And she knew it.

"Well," the priest said, sounding flustered. "Who has the rings?"

"Oh, that's me!" Tasha said, jumping up and fishing down her cleavage for the rings.

"Really?" Annie asked her.

"It was the only place I had. Do you see any pockets in this bitch?" Tasha asked.

Annie closed her eyes, and I laughed.

"Eww, they're warm," Annie groaned, passing hers over to me.

I took it, and slipped it on Annie's finger without waiting for the priest's approval.

"You're mine," I told her.

She grinned, then followed suit, placing the ring on my finger.

"You're mine, too," she informed me.

"Was the priest even needed?" Casten muttered from behind me.

I flipped him off.

"Your tone's not needed," Tasha shot.

"Did I ask you?" Casten shot back.

And things deteriorated from there.

But the main part of the entire thing was accomplished.

Annie was officially *mine*.

***

6 months later

"He got another letter," I said, handing the letter over to Mig.

Mig promptly tossed it into the trash.

I just shook my head, and secretly wished I could make it to where Jennifer couldn't have a pen or pencil anymore.

Any time Mig saw a letter from Jennifer, he got into the worst moods.

Ones that took him hours to work out of his system.

I watched as Mig got up and walked outside, leaving me to finish dinner with Vitaly alone.

"Well," I said to Vitaly. "Would you like anymore pears?"

He slapped the spoon away from me before I could get it any closer to his mouth.

"I'll take that as a no," I said as he babbled and blew spit bubbles.

I handed him his sippy cup that I was trying to introduce him to, and winced when he threw it.

It hit the table with a skid, bounced off the sliding glass window where Mig had just exited, and fell to the floor with a solid crack.

I gathered the dishes, placing them all into the sink and running water over them before I went back to Vitaly with a towel.

Once he was cleaned off, I walked him to his bathroom, and ran a bath for him.

He was playing nicely, making a fantastic mess with bubbles and water, when I looked up to find Mig at my side.

"I'm sorry," he said.

I smiled at him.

"I know."

Mig still didn't like Jennifer any better now than he had six months ago…or even a year ago.

And I knew it would take time for him to get over it, I just wished he didn't close himself off for hours following one of Jennifer's letters.

"I'm gonna go get ready for bed," he said.

I nodded, standing up to offer him a quick kiss.

Which he took and reciprocated.

He gave my butt a soft slap, then exited the room.

I looked over at Vitaly.

"Your daddy's tired," I said. "And you have no water left."

He didn't.

Mostly because it was all over the floor.

Which I left, because I was tired myself.

I'd had a full day at work, having two massage clients, which always drained me, and had done four hair jobs.

It was what you would call, busy.

I never had an uneventful day, and it was getting harder and harder to keep up.

I'd have to hire someone soon, especially if I wanted to keep having Vitaly at the shop with me.

Twenty minutes later, Vitaly was asleep, fed, and a heavy, reassuring weight in my arms.

I laid him down into his crib and smiled at my dog.

She had a new master, and it was most assuredly not me or Mig.

She was all Vitaly's, through and through.

Closing the door quietly, I walked down to our bedroom, not surprised to find Mig already in bed.

He was laying back, the remote in his hand as he flipped through the news stations.

He paused on the one that was showing off a huge bust.

"Hey!" I said excitedly. "You're on the news again!"

He rolled his eyes to me, then shrugged.

He'd had many, many of them over the years.

But his most impressive drug confiscation to date was still the one he'd done with Liam Cornell and his crew.

It'd been a massive shipment of drugs that he'd found after his kidnapping, but this one on the TV was pretty damn impressive in its own right.

"You get him down?" Mig asked.

I went to the bathroom, not bothering to answer his question.

It would be obvious that he was down seeing as he wasn't in my arms any longer.

Vitaly was a momma's boy.

And I was his momma.

Every last bit of myself belonged to him and Mig.

And I was so happy that every day I woke up I was thankful to wake up and experience it all over again.

I was just stepping into the shower when I felt Mig's strong hands on my hips, guiding me in.

His cock...his hard cock...was pressed to my backside as he maneuvered us both underneath he spray of the shower.

"I love you, baby."

I knew he did.

"I know."

He squeezed me tighter, and placed his Jack and Coke on top of the shower stall, right next to my shampoo and conditioner.

This was a nightly ritual now.

I got Vitaly in bed.

He got his drink.

And we met in the shower.

Sometimes we stayed in there long enough to have some hot, steamy sex.

And others we stayed in there until the hot water ran out, talking about our day while he sipped his drink.

"I'm sorry," he said again.

I turned in his arms, studying his face.

The lines that ran out along his eyes.

The hard set of his jaw.

The color of his eyes.

And I fell even more in love with him.

"I know."

"What else do you know?" He asked, teasing me with a kiss on my lip.

"I know that you're mine."

He smiled.

"Damn straight."

ABOUT THE AUTHOR

Lani Lynn Vale is married to the love of her life that she met in high school. She fell in love with him because he was wearing baseball pants. Ten years later they have three perfectly crazy children and a cat named Demon who likes to wake her up at ungodly times in the night. They live in the greatest state in the world, Texas. She writes contemporary and romantic suspense, and has a love for all things romance. You can find Lani in front of her computer writing away in her fictional characters' world...that is until her husband and kids demand sustenance in the form of food and drink.

CPSIA information can be obtained
at www.ICGtesting.com
Printed in the USA
LVOW13s0814261216

518682LV00025B/2261/P

9 781532 766985